The Good Luck Spell

Leanne Tyler

Dedication

To Casey Cothran and Kelly Rivers, I remember fondly the days we spent discussing and plotting this story. Thanks for the great ideas for Vikki.

Other Titles by Leanne Tyler

<u>Anthologies</u>

Through the Garden Gate

<u>Novellas</u>

Ava

It's Always Been You

Victory's Gate

<u>Short Stories</u>

A Country Kitchen Christmas

<u>Novels</u>

Season of Love

The Good Luck Charm

Chapter One

Hearing a knock at her open office door, Jama looked up, shoving the vacation pamphlets she'd been looking at underneath her work. "Lucinda, what brings you here?"

"I hope I'm not interrupting." The Cajun woman walked into the office and closed the door behind her. The jingle of her bangle bracelets chimed as she moved.

"Of course not."

"Good." Lucinda winked and smiled, making Jama feel the woman knew exactly what she'd been browsing.

"Keely asked me to bring you a little present. With the wedding preparations and getting packed for their honeymoon trip, she didn't have time to give it to you herself."

"A present?" Jama's brow rose. "There was no need."

"Yes, but you have agreed to watch Duke and she felt you deserved a little gift."

Jama laughed. Keely obviously didn't know Darren thought he'd bribed her to watch the overweight bloodhound. She couldn't refuse his offer to take over once he and Keely returned from their honeymoon so she could take a long overdue vacation.

"I hope Duke can survive being in my care. Frankly, Lucinda, I know nothing about taking care of a dog, especially one requiring a special diet and exercise routine."

The woman nodded. "Ah, yes, Duke can be a handful. But Keely asked me to give you this business card too. She said if you had any questions or needed help with the dog, you shouldn't hesitate to call Dr. Kyle Landers. He's Duke's vet and a very nice young man, if I do say so."

Jama stood and accepted the card. "Fantastic. I feel somewhat better knowing I'll have someone I can turn to."

Lucinda nodded and motioned to the loveseat and small table. "Do you mind?"

"Of course not. Have a seat. Can I get you anything to drink?" Jama laid the card on her desk and walked over to the loveseat.

"No. I'm fine thank you." Lucinda opened her large black bag and took out an ebony felt pouch and a small spray bottle then patted the cushion next to her. "Come join me."

Jama did as she was asked, watching the woman closely as she pumped the spray bottle, dispersing a fragrance of spice and musk into the air.

"Now, about this gift from Keely."

She slowly nodded wondering why the woman had sprayed incense. "What is it?"

"Something you will find pleasure in." Lucinda's matter-of-fact tone piqued her curiosity further. "I gave this to Keely last year. Come, give me your hand."

Reluctantly, Jama extended her hand, unsure what was going on.

Lucinda chanted an incantation as she slowly parted the pouch's drawstring closure. Then she poured the contents into Jama's palm and closed her fingers around it.

"This is an all-powerful gris-gris. If you wear it around your neck, the amulet will draw your true love to your heart."

"You've got to be kidding!"

The lyrical sound of Lucinda's laughter filled the office. "You sound like my Keely did when I gave it to her. But it is true. You must believe me. How else do you think Darren and Keely worked things out? There were many obstacles, but without this little gem as a guide, I'm afraid Keely would've thrown in the towel too soon and given up on the happily-ever-after she's now found."

Jama glanced toward her office door, glad to see it was closed. She didn't want any of her associates walking by and overhearing this convoluted conversation.

"Now, you may wonder how you will know when you have met your true love. It is easy. The gris-gris will open, spilling forth the blood red stone in his presence once you have opened your heart to the possibilities."

Jama found herself slowly nodding, not believing what she heard. But if what Lucinda said was true ... Things had worked for her brother and Keely. However, she hadn't known the gris-gris played a part in it all.

Slowly she opened her hand and inspected the amulet, noticing the silver filigree securely surrounding the red stone. "You say the stone spills forth? How?"

"It's the magic of the gris-gris. No one knows how this happens. Go ahead, put it on."

"And Keely thinks I need this?" Jama asked, looking at Lucinda.

The woman nodded. "She did discuss it with Darren, and he was in full agreement you were the perfect choice to receive it."

Great! She'd have to remember to thank him when he returned.

Jama shook her head. "I'm sorry, Lucinda, I can't accept this. I'm not looking for a soul mate. I've got my hands full running Wright & Associates."

"Nonsense. Everyone deserves to find happiness in life and working without a little fun is not the way to achieve it. Don't you want to have someone special in your life? Someone to come home to instead of an empty condo?" Lucinda eyed Jama. "Someone you can enjoy going on vacation with?"

A chill ran over Jama at her words and she pursed her lips, shaking her head. She'd only known Lucinda briefly, but she didn't think it entitled the woman to lecture her on the pursuit of happiness. Her mother held that title. Come to think of it, her mother and Lucinda had gotten close during the wedding preparations. She could just imagine them discussing her lack of a social life.

"My grandmother gave me the gris-gris when I was young. I admit I was skeptical, but I wore it. I met my Denton. We had a beautiful life together. You will have one too."

"But—"

"No buts, Jama. Wear it. Take a chance. Who knows what might happen."

She fingered the silver charm, feeling warmth about it as if it were alive. Without thinking, she laid it in her lap; taking the necklace she wore off, she put the gris-gris on. "Okay. I'll give it a try."

Lucinda smiled, standing to go. "Good. Remember, you must wear it every day. I've got a short concert tour in

New England for the next two weeks. I'll be back to check on you, but I have faith you'll be fine."

Jama smiled. "Thanks…I think."

Lucinda winked at her and without another word left the office.

Jama scooped up her discarded necklace before she slowly stood and went back to her desk. Picking up her purse, she dropped the chain into the coin pouch of her wallet before sitting back down at her desk. She picked up a storyboard she'd been reviewing earlier. However, her mind kept wondering to the gris-gris and whether it did have magical powers as the woman claimed. But she knew it would take more than a charm to change her way of thinking. After Ted Donaldson ripped her heart out and stole her blind, putting Wright & Associates in financial straits, she'd vowed never to let another man have control of her life.

She reached for the handset and punched in an extension. "Shelby, the Stanley account is a go. I'm sending the boards to production. Your team did well."

Ending the call, she gathered a few files and stuffed her briefcase, preparing to leave early. Jama couldn't remember the last time this happened, but it would be a norm until the honeymooners returned. Duke was accustomed to being jogged between five and six and she couldn't get him off routine. Darren had insisted she promise to adhere to the schedule.

Dr. Kyle Landers' business card caught her eye and she picked it up, studying it for a moment.

"I hope you're really available if I do need help," she told the card, tucking it in the side pocket of her handbag.

On the way out, she laid the storyboards on her assistant's desk. "Pamela, these are ready for production. Take care of it for me."

"Yes, Ms. Wright. Have a good evening."

Jama smiled. "You too."

Once in her Lexus, she opened the sunroof, letting the breeze blow her hair as she drove to Keely's house. After a quick change she'd take Duke for his daily jog, giving her the rest of the evening to catch up on some files. Or she might call the travel agent back and book her vacation.

Jama pulled into the driveway and she spotted the dog lying under the shade tree. She called to him, but other than look up, he paid little attention to her. Opening the gate, she walked inside the fenced lot and noticed his empty water bowl.

"Someone's been thirsty today." She set her briefcase next to the fence.

The dog moaned.

"Did you say something?"

His eyes closed and his tail flopped back and forth.

"Oh, the silent treatment. I get it. But you do want more water?" She carried the bowl over to the water spigot and turned on the tap. After rinsing it out, she filled it almost full with fresh water and took it back to the shade tree.

The dog instantly came to life and lapped at the water.

Jama stooped down and petted the animal on his head. As if this had all been a test, the bloodhound inched toward her and laid his head on the toe of her shoe. Sticky slobber dripped from his flews, soaking her apricot sling-back, leather pump.

She grimaced at the mess he was making. "No! Not on my new Bini's!"

Duke whimpered, but didn't budge.

"Come on fella, move it," she urged, trying to pull her foot out from under his head. It wasn't an easy task, but she finally managed to get her foot free.

The dog still didn't move and she worried something was wrong. She hadn't been around the dog that much, but she knew he had more life in him than this.

"Duke, what's wrong?"

Concerned the animal wasn't feeling well, she felt of his forehead, then realized what she was doing. "God Jama, what are you doing? He's a dog, not a child."

She wondered how long he'd been without water. She was certain neither Keely nor Darren would leave without making sure he had water, but what if they'd been so busy they'd forgotten? And today had been an unusually warm day for spring, reaching almost into the nineties.

Fearing dehydration, there was only one thing she could do.

Call Dr. Landers.

She fished into the side of her bag for the business card, and turned back toward the dog. "You stay right there. I'll be back."

Jama raced into the house, kicked off her pumps and quickly cleaned off the sticky goo the best she could with a dry paper towel. She'd never thought of herself as the squeamish type, but she shivered as she tossed the used towel into the trash and scrubbed her hands furiously with hot soapy water.

Going upstairs to change, she flipped on the TV and punched in the weather channel number to double check on the temperature before calling the vet. She held the phone between her ear and shoulder while she undressed.

"Eastland Animal Clinic. This is Vikki. Can I help you?" The sound of gum popping echoed across the phone line.

"May I speak to Dr. Landers?"

"I'm sorry, but Dr. Landers had an emergency this afternoon. He's out of the office. If you'd like to make an appointment I can do that for you."

"Um." Her skirt fell to the floor, and she stepped out of it while deciding what to do. "I'm not sure. I'm pet sitting. The dog is acting strange. Moaning. Slobbering. He was without water when I came home today and it got pretty hot."

"Uh huh." Another gum popping sound echoed across the line. "Sounds like an emergency to me. I'll page him. Give me your name and number."

"Jama Wright. 555-7849."

"Pet's name."

"Duke."

"Okay. Got it. I'm sure Dr. Landers will call you as soon as he can. Try to relax. Animals are sensitive and can get agitated easy if they think you're upset."

Jama nodded, listening to the girl's advice. "Good idea. Should I do anything?"

Another gum pop. "Just make him comfortable."

"All right. Thanks."

"No problem. Have a good evening."

The line went dead and Jama put the phone down. She had to relax. Easier said than done when she didn't have a clue what was going on with the dog. She typically wasn't a worrier, but she knew how important the dog was to Keely. He'd become as important to her brother in the last year.

As she changed clothes, she began to wonder if calling the vet over this was jumping the gun, but she felt it was better to play it safe than sorry.

Turning around, she spotted a framed photo of Darren with his arm around Duke on the bedside table. Yeah, she'd be in pretty deep doggie poo if anything happened to that dog while they were on their honeymoon.

She slipped her feet in a pair of athletic mules and went back downstairs, taking the phone with her. From the kitchen window she could see Duke still lying in the shade with his head near the water bowl.

"Poor guy."

She made a quick dinner of a sandwich, some chips, an apple and a bottle of cold water, and headed out to wait for the vet to call her back. She grabbed a blanket on the side porch to sit on.

Kyle Landers flipped his cell phone shut and put the Jeep Wrangler in drive. He had one more stop to make before heading home. Vikki said it might be a false alarm, but he wouldn't leave anything to chance.

Not when it dealt with Duke. The bloodhound had gotten under his skin the last few years.

Kyle recalled Duke's first office visit. He'd been a gangly pup, but that hadn't lasted very long. His owner spent a great deal of time traveling on business and Duke had become overweight. Keely had done a great job stepping in to care for the bloodhound when her brother got transferred and couldn't care for the dog any longer. These days Duke was maintaining his weight, not gaining.

But that still didn't keep Kyle from worrying that the dog would develop bloat. It was a common ailment in deep chested breeds of dogs. And if untreated it could lead to death of the animal. Kyle cared too much for his patients to let that happen.

Half an hour later as the sun began to set, he pulled his beat-up Wrangler alongside the expensive Lexus outside of Keely's house. Apprehension set in, but soon subsided when he spotted a woman sitting on a blanket underneath the shade tree with Duke's head cradled in her lap. She was rubbing his head gently, the way a mother would a sick child.

He sat, watching her in awe until she looked up and caught him. Embarrassed he looked away, grabbing his bag as he got out of the Jeep.

Without him asking the question, she supplied an answer.

"He's resting. Your receptionist said to make him comfortable. I've tried to do that."

"Excellent." Kneeling beside her, he caught the scent of raspberries, and he glanced back up at her. She had the longest lashes he'd ever seen and she worried her lower lip with her teeth while gently rubbing the dog's tummy.

Kyle swallowed hard. "It's the best thing you could have done, Miss. . ."

"Wright. Jama Wright. Nice to meet you." She extended her hand and he shook it.

"Same here. Vikki said you feared he'd become dehydrated. Have you given him water?"

"Yes. But he began moaning, his nose felt wet and his brow felt warm." Her cheeks flushed pink and she shook her head, catching him off guard. She didn't look like the type of woman who'd blush so easy. "I know nothing about taking care of a dog. If anything were to happen to Duke while Keely and my brother are on their honeymoon—"

Kyle held up his hand and stopped her from saying more. "We won't even think along those lines. I don't believe he's dehydrated. His flews are moist, meaning he's producing saliva."

"But the moaning?"

He smiled. "Bloodhounds moan, they slobber. Some of them are very active, others more on the lazy side. Duke prefers the latter. Though I hope he's getting out of the habit with his exercise routine."

She nodded. "Therefore I overreacted."

"It looks that way, but I'll examine him to be on the safe side since I'm here." Kyle reached for his stethoscope and listened to Duke's heart, lungs and stomach. He put on a pair of latex gloves.

She moved away from the dog to allow the vet more room to perform the exam. Duke didn't seem to mind, in fact, he appeared to be enjoying the attention. That is, until the vet applied a small amount of petroleum jelly to a thermometer and inserted it into the dog's backside.

Duke yelped.

"Is that necessary?" Jama winced.

"Yes. I need to check his body temperature."

She frowned, not liking the dog's discomfort. Yet as she watched the Vet's hands gently work with Duke, she could tell he was very concerned for the animal's well being.

"Will he be okay?" she finally asked.

"Yes. I've been concerned for quite some time that he could develop a serious condition known as bloat," he said, rocking back on his haunches. "Some dogs die from it. In more extreme cases, pet owners have chosen for their pets to have surgery to correct the condition."

"Surgery?"

"Yes. But I've been watching Duke closely for the last year because of his weight."

She nodded, listening to the vet explain his diagnosis to her. She couldn't imagine contacting Darren and Keely on their honeymoon to get permission for Duke to have surgery.

"Thank you, doctor, for coming all the way out here to check on him."

"No problem. I'd rather know he's all right than have him suffer until tomorrow." He closed up his bag and got to his feet to leave.

Jama slowly rose, feeling silly. She was always confident and self-assured when it came to business, yet within a matter of minutes Duke had her feeling like a ninny. She didn't even want to think about the impression she'd made on the vet.

"Be sure to call me if you have any questions or notice him acting funny."

"Oh, I will, Dr. Landers. You can be assured I'll call you."

He smiled. "Kyle. Please call me Kyle."

"Okay. Thanks again, Kyle."

He slowly turned to leave and she noticed the way he walked. It wasn't a saunter, but a smooth glide drawing her eye to his hips. He filled out his jeans nicely.

Catching herself staring, Jama gathered the remnants of her dinner and the blanket before she retreated quickly into the house. It had been ages since she found herself interested in a man. What was the matter with her?

A warm sensation flooded her chest area. She reached up and fingered the gris-gris, feeling its warmth.

Lucinda's words ran through her mind. *This is an all-powerful gris-gris. If you wear it around your neck the amulet will draw your true love to your heart.*

Chapter Two

Jama woke to barking the next morning. She jumped out of bed, grabbed her robe and ran downstairs, not taking time to put on her slippers. She was out the back door in seconds, but stopped short when she saw Kyle in the backyard with Duke.

Frowning, she crossed her arms over her chest as she slowly walked to the fence and opened the gate, stepping inside. The wet grass squished between her toes, sending shivers up her spine. She watched as Kyle tossed a Frisbee and then tried to beat Duke to the spot where it landed. His brownish-red hair was damp with perspiration and it curled in little wisps around his face, making him look boyish. Though he was definitely all man – all six foot four inches of him.

Jama swallowed and wet her lips, feeling the gris-gris burn against her throat. She reached up and pulled it away from her skin, annoyed that she'd even accepted it from Lucinda. Somehow that woman had changed her mind about it with a few simple words. Lucinda should have been a salesman instead of a jazz singer.

Duke barked again and Jama looked back up, not believing the change in the dog from yesterday. She'd never seen him more active. Did Kyle have that effect on him?

He sure had an effect on her. She watched his every move, unable to take her eyes off of him as he played with the dog. It seemed so natural for him – as if there was no work to be done, or he didn't have anywhere else to go. He was so carefree. *She'd* be heading into the office in about an hour to catch up on some financial statements and begin research for her next ad campaign. Every second of the day counted in her line of work. She couldn't afford to relax and enjoy a morning playing in the backyard with a dog. And it annoyed her.

"What's going on here?" The chain of the gris-gris turned icy when she called out to him. Startled, she let go and the amulet landed on her chest, chilling her.

Kyle turned at the sound of her voice, breath catching in his throat at the sight of the short, lavender, silk robe she wore. Lace peeked through the v at the neck where the robe criss-crossed in front. Her shapely legs appeared to go on forever. Boy, was he ever a legman.

Warning whistles went off in his head, forcing him to look away and focus on Duke, who was panting at his feet.

"Sure, you can get away with it," he grumbled to the dog.

"Did you hear me?" Jama called, fidgeting with something around her neck.

"Oh, I heard you," Kyle muttered under his breath, letting out a gush of air.

Just look at the dog. Don't look at her. Look at the dog.

How was he going to explain why he was there? Sure he was worried about Duke, but he'd wanted to see her again as well, even if he knew it was dangerous. Since she deserved an explanation, he called to the dog and they jogged over to where she stood.

"I woke early and couldn't stop thinking about Duke so I dropped by to check on him. He seems fine this morning."

"Do you always make unexpected house calls on your patients? And so early in the morning?"

He grinned, daring to look her in the eye. "No. First time, but I like Duke."

She rolled her eyes. "What is it about that dog that makes everyone go gah gah over him?"

"Don't tell me you haven't noticed his charm?" He stooped down and patted the dog on his side. "His droopy eyes. Those wet flews." Kyle cupped the dog's face between his hands.

She shook her head, smiling. "You hungry?"

He laughed, standing back up. "I'm starving."

"I'm afraid I don't cook."

He chuckled, crossing his arms. "For some reason, I had a feeling you'd say that."

She shrugged her shoulders. "I burn water. The kitchen was never an area I excelled in. IHOP's not far from here."

"Okay. Sounds good. Can I wash up?"

Hesitating a moment she finally nodded. "Sure. I guess you're harmless enough. There's a bathroom off the kitchen. Help yourself while I go upstairs and change. I don't think they'd let me in dressed like this."

"Probably not." But he wouldn't mind if they did. He followed her into the house and watched as she hurried up the stairs before going to find the bathroom.

It was around eight that evening when Jama returned home from the office. It had been a horrible day of meetings after long meetings, keeping her at the office longer than she intended. She'd attempted to leave several times so she could take Duke for his scheduled jog, but it hadn't happened. She hated she'd already broken her vow to leave the office by five each day. And now, there was no way she felt up to taking him out for a jog tonight. But she could remedy this. She'd simply get up early in the morning and take him before she went into work.

She dropped a bag of take-out food on the kitchen counter then went out to check on Duke. He was lying in the shade under the oak tree. His head popped up when she came near with his evening allotment of kibble and fresh water. He slowly wagged his tail and crawled over to the bowls without getting up. She'd seen smaller dogs do that, but never a bloodhound. It seemed odd, but she dismissed it since it could easily be something he did often. She watched him eat for a minute before she returned to the house, satisfied that he appeared content.

After eating her own dinner, Jama went upstairs, got ready for bed and settled in for her nightly reading. She went over the prospectus for her next advertising campaign and made a few notes before finally turning out the lights around one. However, an hour later she woke to the screeching sounds of Duke howling. She grabbed her robe and put her feet in her slippers before rushing downstairs.

Her heart pounded and she felt frazzled from being woken so suddenly. She tripped over a small bush going into the fenced-in area and almost fell in her haste. She gazed around the darkened backyard searching for Duke and finally spotted him when the moon came out from behind a cloud. She rushed to the dog and knelt down beside him, rubbing his brow. Still he didn't stop his howling. She rubbed his tummy and his howling subsided into whimpers.

"What's wrong boy?" she asked, recalling how he'd belly crawled to his bowl earlier. Why hadn't she realized then something was wrong with him?

Duke lifted his head. His big eyes looked so sad that she wanted to pull him into her arms and hold him. But she reminded herself he was a dog. *A very large dog.*

"Woooooolf," Duke moaned, rolling over onto his side and stared up at the moon.

Lights went on in the upstairs window at the house next door. She was certain Duke's howling had woken them too. There had to be a way to stop him. But she didn't know how. Her ineptness at taking care of a dog once again surfaced, and she wished she'd begged off when Darren asked her. But in all honesty, he'd made her feel guilty for trying to refuse. After much cajoling they'd come to an agreement. And she felt she was more than earning his covering for her so she could take a vacation.

Jama jumped when a pair of headlights zoomed in on her and Duke. She tried shielding her eyes with the back of her hand, but the bright light prevented her from seeing her visitor. What if the neighbors had called the police because of the noise? Or Animal Control? Somehow from the silhouette of the person walking toward her, she knew it wasn't either, but Kyle before he appeared at the gate, with his vet bag. As he came closer, she saw he wore snug fitting jeans, a white t-shirt and sneakers.

"What are you doing here?" she blurted sounding annoyed, even though she was glad to see him.

"Your neighbors called. I take care of their cats. They knew you were here taking care of Duke while Keely is out of town and weren't sure if you knew how to reach me. I tried calling your number, but didn't get an answer so I thought you might be out here."

Jama nodded, finding it hard to believe he'd jumped into his Jeep and come all the way over because the neighbors had called.

"So you do this twenty-four/seven?" Jama laughed, wondering how many vets in the area made house calls like this. Whatever her previous opinion had been about Kyle Landers, this raised it.

In the dim light, she could see a slight grin appear on his handsome face.

"I care about the animals I treat," he explained as he knelt down beside them. "When did all this start?"

"About half an hour ago I guess." She breathed in his clean scent of soap and spice wondering if he'd just showered. She couldn't take her eyes off him and her pulse quickened. "I'm glad you're here. I don't know what to do with him."

Kyle smiled, slipping on a pair of latex gloves, but his smile faded when in the distance a rumble of thunder sounded.

"Let's get him on the back porch," Kyle suggested.

"Sure," Jama replied, getting to her feet.

Kyle stood and then picked Duke up. He lost his balance and staggered for a moment, then found his footing.

Duke whimpered.

"Careful," Jama warned, leading the way to the house. She opened the screen door to the back porch and turned on the single bulb light. "I think he should be okay here." She pointed to a throw rug.

Kyle laid the dog down as gently as he could manage. "I want you to bring him in to my clinic tomorrow."

"Sure."

"The clinic opens at nine," he added, looking up at her. "Call and set up a time."

She nodded, yawning.

"Why don't you go on up to bed. I'll stay and watch over him for a while," he suggested. "I'll let myself out."

Jama shook her head, yawning again. "No, he's my responsibility. I'll . . ."

"You'll go to bed," Kyle said sternly.

Jama blinked. His voice sounded harsh, but the look in his eyes told of his concern for her. She couldn't remember when anyone had shown her that, especially a total stranger. It felt nice.

"O-Okay," she conceded, half-turning toward the door. She turned back toward him. "But you can sleep on the couch if it gets too late for you to drive home safely."

"Thanks. I might just do that," he said, smiling.

"Goodnight then." Once inside, she retrieved an extra pillow and a blanket from the guest room and placed them on the couch for him before she went upstairs to bed.

Kyle watched as she left, then stretched out on the floor beside Duke. He'd been concerned about the dog when the neighbors called and he'd been just as concerned about Jama. He knew she was nervous about taking care of the dog. Having these unexplainable occurrences wasn't making the adjustment to being a pet caregiver any easier for her.

He wouldn't deny having another opportunity to see her again appealed to him. Their breakfast the other morning had been enjoyable and he'd found himself thinking about her often since then.

He couldn't stop thinking about her soft, blond hair, or how sweet she smelled. He longed to touch more than just her hand. He wanted to pull her into his arms. He wanted to kiss her, to taste her sweetness. However, these thoughts also frightened him. Was he ready to go there again? To open himself up to possible heartache?

Memories of his relationship with Carol two years ago prevented him from freely acting upon his desire. Carol was a dancer. She had been classy like Jama, hair never out of place and her makeup always perfect. She'd been different than any of the women he'd met growing up in Cross Creek.

But Carol had toyed with his heart, pretending to be someone she wasn't, manipulating him into believing she'd be the ideal wife and mother of his children. However, the truth was, Carol wanted nothing more than to get out of Cross Creek, and she saw him as her ticket. The only problem had been that Kyle didn't want the big-life. He wasn't looking to get rich. He'd only wanted to become a vet and care for animals in need. Like Duke and his other patients.

Carol had quickly lost interest in being an animal doctor's wife when Kyle moved to Knoxville to start his practice. Sure, she'd tagged along, talking about a future with him, but she hadn't bothered sticking around. She'd stayed long enough to book a bus ticket to Las Vegas for a career as a showgirl, crushing his perfect image of her and leaving him skeptical of ever getting involved with another woman. He'd been doing just fine keeping that promise until he met Jama.

He glanced over at the now sleeping dog. Whatever had caused the earlier episode had subsided, and it looked like he would sleep through the night. Kyle decided it was time to get some shut-eye too. He didn't think it was wise to leave in case Duke woke and began howling again. Getting to his feet, he turned out the porch light and went into the house.

Kyle found the living room without a problem then settled himself on the couch. He'd catch a little sleep and be gone before morning if Duke didn't have a recurrence. He couldn't risk being there when Jama woke again. He was still trying to get over the memories of her sleep-tousled state.

Jama walked into Wright & Associates and flipped on the lights. As she headed down the hallway to her office, she taped a note to Sue Charles's door, asking Keely's assistant to come see her.

Before she got to her office, however, she could already hear her phone ringing. It was only a few minutes after eight. Why wasn't the answering service taking the call?

Jama reluctantly picked up the receiver. She winced when the service operator informed her that a disgruntled client had been calling. Annoyed, Jama wrote down the number of the client even though this was not the first time he'd called in the last two years. He'd been using every tactic he could think of to get out of his five-year contract.

Jama gritted her teeth, then sat at her desk and pulled the client's file. She jotted down a note of the complaint even though Wright & Associates had fulfilled every inch of the agreement that the client had signed with Ted Donaldson. Ted had been a smooth talker and she knew that was how he got the client to sign the long contract.

Ted. The thought of him made her blood boil. Even after she'd spent two years trying to salvage her business, his sudden departure was still causing her problems. Renewed anger and the pain of betrayal washed over her. She wasn't the type of woman that let her emotions get the best of her, but sometimes she felt so beat down that giving up sounded ideal.

She closed her eyes, leaning her head back against the high-backed office chair. Pinching the bridge of her nose, she wished all thoughts of remorse out of her mind. Giving up was never an option. She was a survivor.

A light knock came at her opened office door.

"You wanted to see me?" Sue asked, holding up the note.

Jama nodded, massaging her temples. "You and Keely are pretty close, right?"

"I like to think so," Sue replied.

"Did she ever mention having problems with her dog Duke at night?"

Sue shook her head and crossed her arms over her chest. "Are you?"

"Yes. Duke's howling and moaning at the top of his lungs. Last night he woke me up. And I'm pretty sure he woke the whole neighborhood."

"Do you think this could be something serious? Did you call the vet?"

"Yes. He came by and Duke's got an appointment later today." She thought about the way Kyle had looked that morning. She'd been pleasantly surprised to find he'd actually slept on the couch last night. He'd looked so good with his shirt off, his feet bare, and the button on his jeans unfastened when she'd walked in on him as he gathered his things to leave. It had been an awkward sixty seconds as they'd both stared at each other, neither saying a word.

Her heart raced at the memory and perspiration broke out around her upper lip. What was it about Kyle Landers that made her senses skitter? Standing up, she quickly took off her suit jacket and unbuttoned the top of her blouse, but she still felt warm from where the gris-gris lay against her skin.

"You know, if I recall correctly, Keely did mention that Duke's vet is very nice looking and he's single," Sue said.

"I wouldn't know," Jama responded, going over to the thermostat and adjusting it. She wished she could take the gris-gris off but recalled Lucinda warning her not to do that. With the way the thing heated and glowed, she didn't want to tempt fate. She didn't think she'd like it turning freezing cold.

"You don't know? Well take a good long look while you're at the appointment. Surely then you can confirm if he's good looking or not." Sue teased, but looked concerned. "Jama? Are you okay?"

"Sure. Why wouldn't I be?"

Sue chuckled. "Because you've got the same look on your face that Keely did after she'd first met Darren. And that girl was smitten. Maybe you are too."

Jama nervously laughed, shrugging. "Nonsense. It's just a little too warm in here."

"Whatever you say." Sue's brow arched. "I've got to get back to work. Let me know how things go . . . with the vet."

Chapter Three

Jama pulled her car into the small parking lot outside of the Eastland Animal Clinic. It was a tiny tan cement building on the south side of town. Glancing nervously back at Duke before putting the car in park, she shook her head in frustration. "I can't believe I rescheduled an important meeting to bring you to the vet, Duke. Who knew taking care of you was going to take more time than I bargained?" She got out of the car and opened the back door.

Duke slowly raised his head. The sad look in his droopy, brown eyes made her cringe. "Oh my gosh, he understood me," she murmured, fastening his leash on him. He couldn't help that he was ill. Fear that she was somehow the cause added to her anxiety.

"Come on, boy, let's go see what the doctor can do for you," she soothed, doing an unladylike squat as she helped him out of the car.

Jama felt out of place in her sharp business suit as soon as she opened the glass door to the clinic. Inside, bright fluorescent lights blinded her for a second. She blinked several times and tried to focus once the spots disappeared.

Duke suddenly pulled on his leash, jerking her further into the waiting area. He barked and lunged, urging her to release him so he could inspect the tiny creatures playing happily in the small pin in the far corner.

"Stop that," Jama commanded, steering him away from the yellow striped kittens. She surveyed the room, taking note of the colorful red, blue, green and yellow Macaw perched on the window ledge, pecking at the bars on the window. Several chairs lined the walls and behind a counter, in the center of the room, sat a vibrant redhead, sporting rows of butterfly clips in her short cropped hair, staring at the monitor of a portable television set.

Jama hesitated a moment when she noticed no one was waiting in the vacant chairs. She looked at the sign on the door again to make sure she was indeed at the right place, then slowly walked to the receptionist.

"Excuse me, I have a —"

"Sh-h-h," the receptionist hissed, waving Jama off.

Jama backed up a step. "Excuse me?"

The receptionist looked up, popped her pink bubblegum then spared Jama a moment. "Sorry, Romey was about to kiss Electra, but they went to commercial. Figures. What can I do for ya?"

"I have an appointment with Dr. Landers."

"What's the name?"

"Jama Wright."

The receptionist scanned a computer printout, running her black painted fingernail down the sheet and shaking her head while mumbling, "Jama . . . Jama . . . Jama. . . No. What's the pet's name?"

Jama pursed her lips in consternation. "Duke."

"Right, here we go. Just have a seat. I'll tell Kyle you're here when the next commercial comes on."

Jama glanced down at her watch and tapped the toe of her designer pump on the tiled floor. "What's your name?"

"Vikki Wood," the girl chirped, popping another bubble.

"V-i-k-k-i. Vikki Wood," the parrot squawked, flying across the room and landing on the counter. He strutted and jerked his head back and forth. "Vikki Wood. Vikki Wood."

"Oh yes, we spoke on the phone." Jama remembered the girl had been more helpful during the call than she was being now.

"Probably."

Jama noticed the obscure writing on the front of the girl's black, cropped t-shirt. *Do you want to seduce me?* was printed in bold, hot-pink letters.

"Do you get many offers?" Jama gestured to the shirt.

"Many offers," the parrot squawked, ruffling his feathers.

Vikki giggled, actually tearing herself away from the TV screen. "All the time. There was a guy with a Komodo dragon in here last week . . . But, there was something about his tongue I didn't like."

"Really? The man's or the dragon's?" Jama couldn't help asking.

The girl frowned, but didn't answer.

"Jama?"

She turned and saw Kyle in his white lab coat coming through a doorway adjacent to the receptionist area. He wore wire-rimmed glasses. A lock of his hair fell haphazardly across his forehead. Her pulse quickened and she took a deep breath. She smiled and the gris-gris burned warm against her chest.

"I hope I haven't kept you waiting too long," he said, glancing over to where Vikki sat with her face glued to the TV screen. He grimaced.

"No, not long at all."

"Well, let's take a look at this fella and see what's wrong with him." He took Duke's leash from her and walked him down a short hallway into the examining room. He led him over to a shiny, four-inch-thick, silver rectangle on the floor, waited for Duke to lie down, and then pressed a button on the wall that caused the rectangle to rise.

"Wow, who would have thought," Jama said out loud, watching the platform ascend to the perfect height for the examining table.

"Yeah I know. New technology is released all the time to improve our day-to-day routines. But this one is all mine. My uncle's an engineer. He designed it for me. It makes getting the larger pets on a table much easier."

"Impressive," Jama said.

"You think so?" Kyle grinned as he put the tips of the stethoscope in his ears.

Jama watched him carefully conduct the examination. She admired the way his hands moved gently, checking first Duke's abdomen, then the dog's mouth. He pushed his flews back so he could see his teeth.

"His gums look normal. He isn't salivating. Has he tried to vomit without success?"

She shook her head.

"Has he been belching gas or vomiting food?"

Jama grimaced. "No. Of course I'm not with him all day because I work. He's just howling and moaning in the evenings for no reason."

"Yeah, that's what puzzles me." His brow creased with concern as he fastened a strap around the dog so he couldn't fall off the table. "I'm hesitant to still think this is bloat, because other than the obvious distress he is in with the howling, the other symptoms are not showing up. But we may only be seeing the first signs because it's in the early stages. If you will agree to it, I'd like to do a blood test, run an ECG and take an X-ray to rule it out completely."

"Absolutely. Whatever it takes to stop his nightly disturbances."

"I can't start him on IV fluids because he doesn't seem to be dehydrated or in shock." Kyle explained as he led Jama back into the waiting area.

"Vikki, can you have Ms. Wright fill out a release form giving permission for treatment of Duke?" he asked.

"Sure," Vikki chirped, reaching for a clipboard and the proper form without moving her eyes off the TV screen.

Jama glanced over the form, signed her name, then handed the clipboard back to Vikki.

"And Vikki, I'll need your assistance," Kyle added, causing the girl to whirl around on the swivel chair.

"Not during *my* stories?" she protested, stomping her foot on the floor.

"Yes, during *your* stories," Kyle said sternly. "Or we'll forget your paycheck this week."

"You wouldn't!" Vikki pouted as she followed him into the examining room. She glanced back at Jama. "Tell me if Drake and Rachel get together. Okay?"

The girl wore tight, hip-hugging black pants that revealed her midriff and the rhinestone, studded belly ring she sported. Jama had never seen an assistant act or dress the way Vikki did. She almost smirked. The girl wouldn't last two minutes if she applied at Wright & Associates. She didn't understand why Kyle put up with her.

Jama sat in a chair and pulled a small portfolio from her briefcase. She went over the paperwork while she waited. However, she found herself becoming more interested in the dialogue of the soap opera that Vikki had been watching than in the proposal. Frustrated, she discarded the paper work and moved to a different location so she could see the TV.

"Pretty lady. Pretty lady," the parrot squawked, ruffling his colorful feathers as he strutted up and down the counter. "Kyle and pretty lady. Kyle and pretty lady."

If only that were true. Where had that thought come from, she wondered.

"Vikki, get Oswald back in his cage," Kyle called, startling Jama. She looked up and caught him staring at her. The smoldering look in his eyes made her skin prickle to gooseflesh.

How long had he been there?

Her breath caught in her throat as their gazes locked and her pulse quickened. Jama didn't understand what was happening to her. Why was she coming unglued over this man she hardly knew? It was so very unlike her. She was acting like she was under a spell or something. Was it the magic of the gris-gris causing this?

She started to ask about Duke, but couldn't find her voice. She moistened her lips, but before she could speak, Vikki whisked into the room, clucking to the parrot. The bird flew to the girl's outstretched arm and plucked a cracker from between her teeth.

Kyle broke his eye contact with Jama and looked at the girl "Vikki, you are the weirdest cousin I have."

She laughed, putting the parrot in his cage. "I'm the only cousin you have, Kyle."

Cousin? So that explained it.

"How's Duke?" Jama finally asked. She was glad Vikki had walked into the room when she did.

"He's doing fine. I gave him a light sedative to keep him calm during the tests. He's sleeping right now," Kyle turned off the television before sitting on the swivel stool and walking it over to where she sat. He took her hands in his. "I don't know how to tell you this, Jama. But my tests and examination show that Duke doesn't have bloat. He's perfectly healthy."

"Oh," Jama said, knowing she should be elated by the news that it wasn't something so serious, but she wasn't. All she could think about was whether she would see Kyle again. The thought that she wouldn't was distressing. "Then why is he howling?"

"Maybe it's separation anxiety?" Kyle shrugged his shoulders and shook his head. "Duke has gone through a transfer of owners twice now. I realize your taking care of him is a temporary situation, but Duke doesn't know that. To him he's been abandoned. Alex left, leaving him with Keely. Now she's suddenly left him with you."

Jama shook her head. "So this could continue until they return?"

"Afraid so."

"Kyle needs a date," Oswald squawked.

Kyle half-grinned. "That bird can be a nuisance."

The bird ruffled its feathers again. "Kyle and pretty lady. Kyle and pretty lady."

Jama glanced down and saw he still held her hands and Vikki was nowhere in sight. They were alone. Besides the parrot and the playful kittens, she was absolutely alone with Kyle Landers, Duke's too sexy vet. Her pulse quickened and she couldn't remember the last time she had felt so rattled. She wanted this man to kiss her and that thought scared her.

"I guess I should get Duke and go," she forced herself to say.

"There's no rush. He's still sleeping," Kyle said, his pant leg brushed against her thigh.

A jolt of electricity soared through her. She couldn't stop looking into his mesmerizing green eyes, or ignore her light-headedness. She closed her eyes for a second to clear her head. Thoughts of the unfinished work waiting on her desk back at the office flitted across her mind, but she tried to push them away. She really wanted to stay here with him instead of rushing off. For once, she wanted to be carefree, but her sense of responsibility to her business nagged at her. Finally, she found her resolve and opened her eyes.

"I really should get back to work."

Kyle swallowed hard, letting go of her hands and sat back on the stool. *What was he thinking? He'd been inches away from kissing her.* "I'll bring Duke home later. There's no way you'd be able to get him in or out of the car with him sedated."

"Sure," Jama agreed, reaching into her bag for the car keys. She stood and he did the same. There was an awkward silence as he followed her out to the Lexus.

"We'll bill you for the procedures today," he said for lack of anything better though he could care less about the money. He was glad to know the dog was fine.

"Thanks for everything," Jama said, getting into the car. She waved, then pulled out of the lot.

He watched as her car disappeared down the street before finally going back inside the clinic.

"So you got a thing for her?" Vikki asked, pushing a broom across the clinic floor.

"What makes you ask that?" he grunted.

"Oh, the way you looked at her. The way you talked to her and held her hands." Vikki leaned against the broom handle. She waved her hand over the floor. "Your sudden need for me to clean the waiting area."

He shrugged his shoulders. "So what? What does any of that have to do with Jama? The floor needed to be swept."

"Right." Vikki laughed. "I can see it now. You'll be sitting by the phone tonight hoping that dog starts his bellyaching cries again just so you can go to her side. Mark my words. You've got it b—a—d."

Kyle grunted again and walked to his office to finish the paperwork for Duke's file. Who would have thought his flaky cousin would notice his reaction to the "pretty lady?" And if Vikki saw it, did that mean Jama had too? Was that why she'd been in such a rush to leave?

She's city. You're country. What makes you think she'd give you a second thought?

"Because I want her to," he admitted, shutting his office door.

Chapter Four

Jama finished work early so she'd be waiting at home when Kyle brought Duke. She wanted to invite him to dinner. It was the least she could do. After all, he'd come by to check on the dog more than once this week, and he'd even gone out of his way to bring Duke home so she wouldn't have to deal with a sedated dog. Her only problem was the cooking bit. She'd have to pick up takeout.

She had no idea what Kyle liked to eat, other than at breakfast. His choice of bacon and sausage with his pancakes at IHOP the other morning made it clear he wasn't a vegetarian. But did he have a favorite type of food?

Almost everyone she knew liked Chinese, and she knew the best place to get takeout. Swinging by the Flaming Dragon, she got their Hunan special which had chicken, beef, pork, and seafood in it, crab fried wontons, vegetable lo mien and a pot of green tea. Feeling certain she'd selected a good variety, she headed home.

Kyle pulled in behind her when she arrived at the house on Cedar Lane. Duke's head appeared at the side widow of the Jeep, and he wagged his tail when she got out of her car.

"Hi," she called out. "How's Duke doing?"

Kyle smiled, stepping down from behind the wheel. "He's doing okay. Didn't have any side effects from the sedative, which is good. I took him for his jog before we headed this way."

"Really? Oh that's great. Thanks. I really owe you big time now," she said, charging ahead with her invite. "I picked up dinner for two hoping you'd be able to stay. Can you?"

"You did?"

She nodded. "You've been a lifesaver for me this week. I'd be going crazy right now trying to figure out what to do with Duke if it hadn't been for your house calls. I can't thank you enough."

"I appreciate your appreciation, but I care about animals. That's why I'm a vet. Thanking me isn't necessary. Wait till you see the bill."

She laughed. "True, but—"

"Jama, I accept your invitation to dinner. Let me put Duke in the fence and I'll be right in."

"Great. I'll set the table." She stepped up to the Jeep and cupped Duke's face in her hands. "I'm so glad you're okay, fella."

Duke whimpered and tilted his head toward her as her hands moved away.

"I think he likes you."

"Really?"

"Yeah. He wagged his tail when you spoke to him."

Jama thought about that as she got the takeout bags out of the car. She'd developed a soft spot for the dog too, but she wasn't about to admit it. "I'll see you inside."

Kyle watched her walk toward the house. She had a nice sway to her hips and he liked the way her suit skirt danced around the calves of her legs when she walked.

Duke barked as if in agreement.

"Yeah, you can say that again." He turned toward the dog and fastened his leash before helping him down. "Let's get you settled in your lot with fresh water and some kibble."

With the dog taken care of, Kyle went back to his Jeep, and checked his shirt for odor. He didn't want to offend her after he'd been jogging so he pulled out the clean shirt he kept on hand for unexpected accidents. The soiled shirt went into the back seat of the vehicle. He slipped the clean one over his head and walked toward the house. He rapped on the screen door; then when she motioned to him, he went on in.

"Hmmm, something smells delicious."

"It does. I hope it tastes as good."

"I'll wash up quickly then and we'll see."

"You remember where the bathroom is?"

"Yeah, I'll be just a minute." He went down the small hall to the bathroom and turned on the water.

"I have green tea, chilled water, or soda. What do you prefer to drink?" she called from the kitchen.

"Water's fine." He washed his hands, then ran them wet through his hair so it didn't look so windblown. Washing his hands again, he dried them quickly and returned to the kitchen.

"I took a gamble that you'd like Chinese," she said sitting down.

"I eat it occasionally, though back home we were raised on meat and potatoes."

"Where's home? Aren't you from Knoxville?"

"No, born and raised in Cross Creek. I only came here after finishing vet school."

Jama nodded, offering him the bowl of rice. "I don't believe I know where Cross Creek is located."

"Back country of Middle Tennessee. Small community with an established vet, so there wasn't a need for another."

"What made you decide on Knoxville?"

Kyle selected a few pieces of meat from the platter. "Well, my uncle and his family live here, so I figured having family close by wasn't a bad idea."

"The engineer?"

"Yeah, Vikki's dad."

She picked up a bowl and offered it to him. "Vegetable lo mien?"

"Thanks."

"You two seem very different."

Kyle laughed. "That's an understatement, but I guess it goes to show the impact different environments and exposures can have on a person."

She nodded. "Plus, Vikki is much younger than you."

"Definitely." The first bite of chicken made his eyes water and his mouth burn, and he reached for his glass of water. "Jama, this is spicy."

"It's Hunan. You like it?"

"Hunan. Is that a type of spice?"

"More like a combination of spices. Chili peppers, garlic, shallots."

He coughed. "Chili peppers?"

"Yes, why?"

"I think you better take me to the ER. I'm allergic to chili peppers."

"Allergic?" She bumped the table standing up quickly.

Kyle coughed again and reached for his water. He'd only eaten a small amount but he could already feel his throat tightening. "Yes. Now."

"Oh my God!"

"Don't panic," he warned, getting up from the table. "It won't do either of us any good."

Jama grabbed her purse and flipped off the lights, as they went out the door. She ran ahead of him to the car, opening the passenger side door. Once he was inside, she ran around to the driver's side and jumped behind the wheel.

"I'm sorry, Kyle. I never dreamed —"

"Just drive Jama, we'll worry about this later." He voice was low and his face was ashen.

"Right."

She started the motor and turned the car around before pulling out of the drive. They were only ten minutes, at the most, away from the nearest hospital. All she could think about was killing him with her choice of spicy Chinese food. Food allergies had never crossed her mind.

Kyle turned the air conditioning higher as she drove and she noticed he was looking rather pale. She punched the button for the emergency flashers and drove faster when possible and changed lanes often. Finally arriving at the ER entrance, she pulled to a stop and rushed inside to get help.

An EMT followed her back out with a gurney. He moved Kyle quickly to the bed and checked his vitals.

"Just hang on, Kyle," she urged following along beside them.

"You'll have to move the car," the EMT said, rolling him into the emergency room.

Jama stopped short of the sliding doors, feeling numb as the adrenaline rush slowly subsided. "Right."

She walked back to the car and shut the passenger door before getting behind the wheel. None of this would have happened if she could cook.

No? You could have given him food poisoning instead. "Ugh." The alternative wasn't any better.

A policeman stopped her as she entered the ER again. "The doctor would like to speak with you. He's with your husband in room four."

"Oh, and I'll need you to fill out some paperwork," the lady behind the counter said.

Jama nodded, then started to protest when it registered what the officer said. "But—"

"Room four."

Opening the door, she spotted Kyle leaning back against the elevated bed, his shirt cut open, exposing his chest. An oxygen mask covered his nose and mouth and several wires ran to the monitors behind the bed keeping track of his vital signs. His eyes were closed so she didn't know if he was resting or unconscious.

The doctor looked up from the chart he was filling out. "Ah, good, you're back."

"How is he?"

"Better than when you brought him in. Timing is everything when a person goes into anaphylactic shock."

Anaphylactic shock?

Jama sank into the chair near the door feeling as if her legs wouldn't support her. "Will he be okay?"

"Yes, in a few hours he'll be fine. We've given him an injection of epinephrine to open up the airway in the throat and his blood vessels. I'd like to keep him for observation until I feel he's stable enough to go home."

She nodded. "I did this to him."

"Exactly what did you do?"

She looked up at the doctor. "I poisoned him."

Chapter Five

"Would you mind repeating that?" the doctor asked, walking toward her.

"I fed him Hunan, not knowing he was allergic to chili peppers." She fingered the gris-gris, feeling its warmth as she talked. "I could have killed him."

The doctor laughed. "You're kidding."

"I don't think it's funny," she snapped, not understanding how a medical professional could find humor in the situation. After all, she'd picked up Chinese to avoid a possible trip to the ER because she couldn't cook. The irony of it all didn't set well with her.

"No, it's not," the doctor coughed, "but your earlier statement sounded like you intentionally tried to murder him."

Jama sucked in her breath. "Oh. No. Never," she quickly said. "Well...not intentionally. But it could happen."

"It could?" The doctor raised a brow.

She nodded, staring at Kyle's seemingly lifeless body lying on the gurney. "If I really tried to cook for him, it could be disastrous. I'm a whiz in the boardroom, but keep me out of the kitchen."

"I see." The doctor cleared his throat. "Can you at least use a microwave?"

"Of course I can," she retorted. "I'm a successful business woman who isn't domesticated, but I'm not completely helpless."

"That's good. At least you don't have to rely on takeout for all your meals. As a doctor, that would concern me. But you do look healthy."

The doctor's comment made her squirm in her chair and she frowned, glancing at him. He looked like he wasn't in tiptop shape himself. So where did he get off lecturing her on her eating habits? "I am healthy. My doctor gave me a clean bill of health last week. And to answer your question, no, I don't *only* eat takeout."

"Can he cook?" The doctor motioned toward the gurney.

"I guess." She bit her bottom lip as she once again stared at Kyle lying motionless in the hospital bed. "Are you sure he's going to be all right?"

"Yes. He'll be fine." The doctor wrote something in the chart. "Try not to worry."

She nodded, stood, and walked to the bedside. She laid her hand on Kyle's and it felt warm. A half drained IV bag hung at the side of the bed. She'd never experienced anything as scary, even when she took care of her younger siblings growing up. She knew now she'd been very lucky and was so thankful Patti and Claire loved to cook.

"If it makes you feel better, most newlyweds go through similar mishaps. I'm sure you'll eventually learn to cook. Most women do."

Jama spun around. "But we're not married. Why would you think that? We're not even dating. Probably never will now."

The doctor looked shocked by her statement. "If you're not family, then I'm going to have to ask you to go back to the waiting room. It's hospital policy. Only family members can accompany patients to the examining area."

"Leave him? I can't possibly. What if he needs something? Or has another reaction?"

"That's unlikely, we're monitoring his vitals. But if it makes you feel better I'll have a nurse check on him often."

Jama shook her head and grabbed the doctor's arm. "Listen, you don't understand. He's my sister-in-law's vet. He's practically lived at the house this week because her bloodhound is moaning and groaning for no reason. I'm a business woman. I've never owned a pet. I don't know anything about taking care of dogs." She looked back at the bed. "I'll go out of my mind if something should happen to Kyle. That's why this all happened. I wanted to thank him for his help. Only I picked the wrong food."

The doctor looked at her as if she'd just grown a second head. Jama released his arm and stepped back. *Oh my God. He must think I'm losing it. He'll be calling the Psych ward for an evaluation if I don't shut up.*

Silence filled the room and she tried to calm down. But she couldn't stop worrying about Kyle.

The doctor shook his head. "I understand how you feel, but hospital policy dictates in these situations. If I knowingly allowed you to stay and someone found out—"

Kyle heard Jama's voice, but she sounded miles away. Rubbing his face, he felt hard plastic covering his mouth and nose. He removed the oxygen mask and tried to open his eyes. His eyelids were heavy, making it difficult to open them. When his vision cleared the first thing he saw was her back and the curve of her bottom. He smiled and tried to sit up, but he felt woozy.

"I'm not leaving," she said.

Leave? No. She couldn't leave. He needed her.

"Jama, don't go." His voice sounded barely above a whisper and he didn't know if she'd heard him.

"Kyle?"

His vision blurred again, watching her turn around. "How's my little dog sitter doing?"

A frown creased her pretty brow as she stepped closer to the bed. Her hand touched his forehead and he found pleasure in that momentary touch.

"Kyle. Oh Kyle, I'm so sorry." She leaned over him.

"It's okay, honey. I'll live. You can't get rid of me that easily."

"I wasn't trying to."

"I know." He brushed a stray lock of hair away from her cheek, wanting to pull her to him and kiss her.

"How are you feeling, Mr. Landers?" the doctor asked, causing Jama to move away from him. "Do you notice any side effects lingering from the chili peppers?"

Kyle shook his head and cleared his throat. "No doc. I think I'll live. I want Jama to stay, don't make her go."

"Mr. Landers—" the doctor began.

"She stays."

"If you insist, but I'm making a note of this in your chart."

"I do insist. When can I go home?"

"I'd like you to stay at least another hour for observation." The doctor wrote something before he looked back up. "If your vitals stay the same, I may release you before then."

"Fair enough."

The doctor hung the chart at the end of the bed. "I have other patients to see to. I'll be back."

Jama's brow arched when the door closed. "Well, how do you like that? He wouldn't relent to me, but you—"

"I'm the patient. He has to make me happy to some extent."

"Is that so?"

"Yeah," Kyle said, scooting over to make room for her to sit on the edge of the bed. He patted the spot. "Sit."

Jama's brow arched again, but she did as he asked. He reached for her hand, rubbing his thumb across her palm.

"I'm sorry I ruined your dinner."

"Sorry? You? I'm the one that's sorry. This was way too scary. If you'd died—"

"But I didn't. You got me here in time."

"But what if I hadn't? I couldn't have stood losing you. I may never eat Chinese again."

He laughed, breaking the serious moment even though he wondered if she really meant it the way he hoped. "There's no need for that."

"Are you allergic to anything else?"

"No. As far as I know chili peppers is the only thing that causes a reaction."

"Good. I don't want to go through this again."

He laughed. "Believe me, honey, I don't want to go through it again either."

She finally smiled, tilting her head to the side. "Did you know you've called me honey twice now?"

"Have I?"

She nodded.

"Is that bad?"

She shook her head. "No. Actually, I find it's nice."

"Good." He leaned forward, placing his hand at the back of her neck, pulling her to him and brushed his lips against hers. She leaned into him for a moment, returning the kiss before she abruptly pulled away.

Her cheeks flushed. "What was that for?"

"For not killing me."

Chapter Six

Jama thought about Kyle's kiss for the next two days. Every time she did, her stomach did flip flops like when she was a teenager. She didn't understand why a simple kiss was affecting her this way. After all, she'd been kissed and more before.

But not by anyone like Kyle. And not after she'd sent him to the ER.

Her love life was extinct. She didn't date anymore. And her past history was near to none. In high school she'd briefly dated the captain of the football team, Scott Branson, until she found out all he wanted was a passing grade in economics. Then in college she'd dated a graduate student in business. Their relationship had gotten intimate, but ended after a year when both realized they spent more time pursuing their degrees than each other.

"Then there was Ted." She groaned at the memory of him. To date, her relationship with him had been the longest. Three years, five days and twelve hours. She knew the exact time when it ended. Precisely at noon when she'd received the call from him before he boarded a plane to destinations unknown.

She'd never had a happy ending. Perhaps that's why she didn't believe in Lucinda's gris-gris. The cards were stacked against her.

She stared in the mirror of her compact at the charm, noticing the intricate design and wondered how it could open when the edges of it were smooth.

"That's the magic of it," Lucinda had said.

Jama still doubted the amulet had any powers at all. Of course it did become warm at the oddest times and only when Kyle was around. Had that been the way it had worked for Keely? Had her sister-in-law been as confused by it as she?

Kyle. Thinking about him made her smile. He'd started calling her honey and she liked the endearment even if it possibly didn't hold any meaning. Other than the little kiss he'd not shown any real interest in her. Had he? He came over often, but that was to check up on Duke, not to see her. Or was that just a pretense?

"It's been so long I don't even know," she mumbled to herself, snapping the compact closed. Putting it in her purse, she rearranged the papers on her desk trying to find her pen.

"Did you say something, Jama?" Sue Charles asked, walking by her opened office door.

"I was talking to myself."

"Oh, okay. How's Duke doing?"

"About the same. He still moans and groans, but as long as I pay lots of attention to him or Kyle comes over to see him, he seems to be doing okay. I might survive the next two weeks until Darren and Keely return."

"Wonderful!" Sue cheered.

"Is it?"

Sue gave her a puzzled look. "Kyle's the vet, right?"

"Yeah."

"He's coming over regularly?"

"Yes."

She grinned. "Looks like catching Keely's bridal bouquet is bringing you some unexpected luck in the male department."

"Ha." Jama had forgotten about catching that darn bouquet. Between it, the gris-gris and the way she felt about Kyle, she had three strikes against her. If she wasn't careful she'd start believing in happily ever after.

"Don't go trying to read between the lines, Sue. The only *mail* I'm interested in is the kind the postman brings."

Sue shook her head. "If you say so. See you around."

"If you say so," Jama mimicked when she was certain Sue was out of earshot. That girl was always too perky for her own good. But she liked her and was glad Jackson and Jackson had agreed to allow Keely to take her assistant with her when she left their employment and came to work at Wright & Associates.

What burned Jama the most was she liked Kyle and she knew it. She could pretend otherwise to Sue and everyone else, but she had to be honest with herself. He was nothing like Ted or any man she'd dated before and that was what worried her. Kyle was the outdoorsy type. His choice of vehicle spelled that out loud and clear. And the way he dressed. Not once since she met him had she seen him wearing anything other than broken-in jeans and a T-shirt, or a button up polo.

He's easy going. Animals love him.

She was all work and no play. She'd conditioned herself to that lifestyle at an early age. After their father walked out, it had been her responsibility to look after Claire, Patty and Darren while her mother worked two jobs. Her friends thought she was a drudge spending all her free time studying instead of going out and having fun. But she'd never resented all the social events she'd given up.

This conditioning had led her to excel in high school in order to receive a full scholarship to the local university where she carried a double major in advertising and business. She'd studied hard those four years while working a part-time job, allowing her to save for graduate school.

"I run an accomplished advertising company and I just celebrated my thirtieth birthday. Not many people can claim that."

A tap came at her door and she looked up to see Judith, her accounting supervisor. "Do you have a minute?"

"Sure. Come on in."

Judith carried two steaming mugs of coffee and clutched a manila folder under one arm. She closed the door with her hip.

"What's up?"

"It's the Heavenly Baby Products account Darren landed." Judith handed her a mug of coffee.

"I thought everything was going smoothly."

"Same here, but I received a rejection letter from Templeton himself on the first invoice. He is refusing to pay because he said Darren verbally agreed —"

Jama held up a hand and stopped Judith in mid-sentence. "No. No. We don't do verbal agreements." She reached for the letter and read over it. "Let me go pull Darren's copy of the contract."

She went down the hallway to her brother's office and unlocked the door. Flipping on the overhead light, she went to the lateral file cabinet and searched for the paperwork in question. Skimming the contract, she found the passage she was hoping to find. Closing the drawer, she walked to the doorway, flipped off the lights and shut the door behind her.

Returning to her office a few moments later, she smiled. "The man doesn't have a leg to stand on. Darren's copy of the contract spells out the agreement they made clearly. Templeton signed it himself. I'll give the man a call about this and see if we can get him to pay the invoice when Darren gets back from his honeymoon."

"That'll be fine. I wanted you to be aware of what's going on before I rebilled." Judith settled back in the chair and sighed. "How are you? I haven't seen you all week."

"I've been here," Jama assured her.

"I didn't doubt it. You're always here." Judith sipped her coffee. "Have you thought about taking a vacation this year?"

Jama nodded. "Yes. I plan to before the end of the summer."

"Fantastic. I know it's been over two years since you took any time off. After the incident with Ted you turned into a workaholic. But when Darren joined the agency and then Keely came, I thought perhaps you'd begin to back off a little. Put your needs before the company's. I haven't seen that and I'll admit, I've been worried about you."

"Lots of things changed after Ted left," Jama remarked, reaching for a sticky note.

"They sure did. And not always for the better." Judith looked concerned. "Do you even date anymore? What do you do for fun? You're always at the office by eight if not before and you're usually here way after I leave at six. I even suspect you come in on the weekends."

Jama frowned. "Are you keeping tabs on me?"

"Anyone who works here knows the life you lead. We don't have to keep track of your comings and goings. It's a well known fact."

She took a deep breath. "Judith, I've always valued our working relationship and friendship. If I want to hear all of this, I'll call my mother. I don't need to hear it from you too."

Judith held up her hand. "I'm concerned about you. That's all. You know what they say. All work and no play makes Jama a dull woman."

Dull? Did people see her that way? She rested her head in her hands for a moment before running her fingers through her hair.

"When's the last time you took a day off because you could?" Judith's question made her look up again. "Did you ever play hooky from school?"

She shook her head.

"Maybe it's about time," Judith suggested, getting to her feet before she left the office.

Hooky? Did she dare?

An image of herself and Kyle lounging on a catamaran near the British Virgin Islands flashed through her mind. Kyle tanned, his hair wet and sun streaked. How she'd love to spend a week or more on a boat with him.

The phone ringing startled her and she jumped, knocking her coffee cup over. Black liquid splashed all over the papers on her desk and her white linen suit.

"Damn!" She jumped up from the chair, grabbed the papers and tried to salvage them from the spill. The phone continued to ring and she grabbed at it, but whoever was calling hung up as she put the receiver to her ear.

"Great!" She slammed the handset down and grabbed a wad of facial tissue from the box on her desk to blot the wet stain on her suit.

Without allowing herself to think, she picked up her purse and left her briefcase beside the desk. She closed the door behind her. "I'm leaving for the day, Pamela."

"You are?" Her secretary chirped. "But—but it's not even ten."

Jama smiled. "Amazing isn't it?"

"Y-yes. Yes it is. Have a good day, Ms. Wright."

"I plan on it."

Kyle hung up the phone disappointed and checked the number before he dialed again.

"Whatcha doin'?" Vikki asked, coming into his office.

"Making a phone call." He hung up the phone, not wanting her to see the number he'd been dialing on the digital display. His cousin had been riding him pretty hard about his obvious interest in Jama Wright. He usually could take ribbing of any kind, but he didn't like it where Jama was concerned.

"You have a new patient out in the lobby," Vikki said, rocking back on her heels. "He's really big."

"Big?" Kyle asked.

"*Real* big." Vikki emphasized with her hands.

"Hm-m-m."

She fidgeted with her hair, tousling it. The color of the day was the dark brown she only chose a couple times a year. Then she repositioned the elastic neckline of her white eyelet top, baring her shoulders and tugged her peasant style skirt down a little to show off her midriff. She removed the ever-noticeable rhinestone, studded belly ring and slipped it into the pocket of her skirt.

Kyle blinked, amazed at what he was seeing. He'd been trying to get her to stop dressing outrageously since she started working for him. He didn't understand what had gotten into her.

"You know once you take those out you can't put them back in. What's up with you?" He pushed away from the desk before heading out of his office.

"Nothing."

Kyle didn't believe it for a second, but he didn't question her further. Whatever had caused the change in her was fine with him. However, he immediately understood when he walked into the waiting area of the clinic.

A tall young man dressed in jeans, boots, a button-up shirt and a cowboy hat completely blocked the doorway and standing next to him was his horse.

His horse? Vikki's emphasis with her hands flashed before his eyes.

"I'm Dr. Landers. How can I help you?"

"Kit Blankenship." The cowboy extended his hand. "Jasper became ill somewhere between here and Nashville. We've been on the road for the last month riding with a small rodeo circuit, raising money for different charities. I was told you're the best."

"Isn't he magnificent?" Vikki purred, sashaying up to the horse. She wore the perfect smile.

The horse or his owner? Kyle wondered. The obvious alterations to her appearance were not unnoticed either.

"Thank you, ma'am," Kit said, tipping back his hat and grinning. "You're a fine looking filly yourself."

Vikki giggled and her cheeks flushed pink.

Kyle blinked. Vikki blushing? He cleared his throat. "Vikki, take Jasper back to exam room four. I'll be back shortly."

"Certainly," she replied, taking the reins from Kit. She was halfway across the room when she stopped, turned and asked, "Is exam room four large enough?"

"Yes."

Kyle waited until Vikki was out of sight before he questioned Kit further about Jasper's condition. He didn't want the girl causing distractions.

"You said Jasper is ill. In what way?"

"He isn't eating. He's irritable," Kit replied.

"Is he drinking water?" Kyle asked, reaching for a clipboard on Vikki's desk.

"Not his normal amount. That's what worries me. I'm afraid he'll come down with the colic if it continues," Kit said, taking his Stetson off and running his hand over his dark head of curls.

"How long has his water intake been low?"

"A day or two."

"And how long have you been on the road traveling?" Kyle asked, writing this all down on a notepad he pulled from his coat pocket.

"Three weeks now."

Kyle nodded and handed Kit the clipboard. "Fill out these forms and I'll go take a look at Jasper."

Kyle left him in the waiting area and headed down the hallway to the exam room hoping nature's call hadn't caused Jasper to have an accident. He wasn't equipped for horses to visit his facility. He normally made farm visits instead.

"Vikki, cover the floor in newspaper for me," he said, walking into the exam room. He grabbed a pair of latex gloves from the supply cabinet before he began the exam.

"Newspaper?" Vikki questioned. "He's a horse, Kyle. Not a puppy."

Kyle let out a jagged breath. "Just do it. We don't have any straw, meaning we'll have to improvise."

"Whatever," she said and disappeared.

A few minutes later, Kyle emerged from the exam room to find Vikki ogling Kit as they made small talk.

"How is he?" Kit jumped up from the chair where he sat.

"Fine from what I can tell. He doesn't have colic. He does appear to have gotten some bad feed. That may have happened at your last stop. There could have been a little mold in it. Don't be alarmed. Checking the feedbag you use can prevent it. Clean it out and begin with a combination of leafy Alfalfa and some orchard grass. Since you are from out of town I called a local farm where I do regular visits and Mr. McDougal said you can bring Jasper over to graze at no charge. They'll even put the horse up for the night." Kyle handed him a slip of paper with directions on it. "I got him to drink water. Take it slow with the intake as if he'd been overheated. I'll be out tomorrow morning to check on you."

Kit nodded. "Thanks."

"No problem. Vikki will get you all set up with further directions and a map of the area. She might even agree to tag along to show you where the farm is located."

"I'd be glad to if you like," she said, sounding nonchalant.

"S-sure, that would be good," Kit said, folding the directions and slipping them into his shirt pocket. "Can I see him now?"

"Go ahead." Kyle nodded.

Vikki grabbed Kit's hand. "Come on, I'll show you."

Kyle waited until they were out of sight then walked over to the reception desk. He picked up the phone and dialed Jama's office number again, amazed to realize he'd already memorized it.

"Wright & Associates. Can you hold?" a female voice answered.

Light tempo music played over the line as he waited. He flipped through his appointment book and saw his afternoon was free. But when wasn't that the case? He needed to find a way to drum up business. He hated to think of the consequences if it didn't pick up.

He sat down in Vikki's chair and started straightening up the desk. She'd been going through the mail, stacking the bills in one pile and sorting the remainder. An unopened envelope addressed to him caught his attention and he pulled it out of the stack. He was about to open it when the voice came back on the line.

"Sorry to keep you waiting. How can I help you?"

"Jama Wright please."

"I'm sorry, but Ms. Wright is out of the office for the rest of the day. Can I take a message?" the female asked without skipping a beat.

"No. No message. Thanks." He hung up and immediately dialed Keely Jones' number on the chance Jama had gone to the house. He didn't expect her to be there, but he gave it a try anyway. She was probably in a meeting across town. He could imagine her dazzling a client with her smile and of course, the presentation.

The line rang once, then twice before the answering machine picked up. A perky duo greeted him. "Hello, you've reached the Wright's, Keely Jones and Darren. We're unable to take your call right now, please leave us a message. And if you're trying to reach Alex, well, he left the country."

Kyle hesitated about leaving a message as the beep sounded. He didn't know if Jama would be checking the machine. But other than stopping by to check on Duke, he hadn't spent much time with her since the trip to the ER and their chaste kiss.

He decided to take the professional approach. "Hi, Jama, it's Kyle. I'm calling to see how Duke's doing. I tried you at work, but you weren't in. Call if you need anything. You've got my number."

Jama walked in the back door and heard Kyle's voice. At first she was confused, and then she realized what she heard was the answering machine. She raced toward the phone on the kitchen counter, but by the time she reached it the line went dead.

"Damn." She hit the counter with her hand. Twice in one day she'd missed a call. Both from Kyle she bet. She punched the answering machine and replayed the message, savoring the sound of his voice.

Her spirits lifted and she knew how she was going to spend the rest of the afternoon. For the first time in her life she was going to play hooky and she hoped Kyle would agree too.

Chapter Seven

Jama ran up the stairs and changed out of her ruined linen suit, wishing the dry cleaners could do miracles and remove the coffee stain. Then she searched for the right outfit to wear. Half an hour later dressed in casual slacks and a summer weight sweater set, she headed to the Eastland Animal Clinic, hoping to surprise Kyle.

She parked and got out, noticing the lot void of cars. The same as it had been on her first visit. She opened the door and went inside. When her eyes adjusted to the change in light, she saw Vikki's desk vacant. The only thing stirring in the waiting area were the playful kittens in the corner.

"Kyle?"

"Kyle." Oswald squawked amid a flurry of colorful feathers as he glided into the waiting area and landed on the counter. He strutted, jerking his head back and forth, ruffling his feathers and whistling at her.

Jama jumped and her heart fluttered. "Silly bird."

"Sorry. I was cleaning his cage and he got away from me." Kyle followed after the bird and hung the cage on its stand. When he opened the door, the parrot flew inside and perched on the swing. "Where's Duke?"

"I left him at home."

He nodded. "Is everything okay?"

"Yeah. He's doing well for now."

"That's great. Maybe that means he's finally adjusting to having you take care of him."

"I can only hope." She smiled.

"So what brings you by?" He leaned on the counter.

"I got your call. Sorry to have missed you."

"No problem. I just wanted to check on him."

"Is that all?" she asked, seeing the small talk was getting them nowhere.

He nodded. "Why aren't you at work?"

"Bad morning. Decided I needed some time away from the office. It feels kind of strange to take the day off. I don't really know what to do with myself."

Kyle laughed. "Foreign territory?"

"Totally."

"Hmmm…if it were me, I'd head to the mountains for some hiking. But I see from the look on your face that isn't very appealing."

She shook her head. "No. I don't think I'd want to do that alone. That would definitely be a two-person adventure."

"Okay, what would you enjoy doing?"

He straddled the desk stool and motioned for her to sit in the adjacent chair.

'Anything that involves you' was on the tip of her tongue, but Jama couldn't bring herself to say it. Instead she said, "First off I'd like to have lunch. Have you eaten yet?"

Kyle inched the rolling chair away from her. "Oh no. I don't think we want to go there. The last time wasn't pleasant."

She laughed. "I would let you pick the restaurant."

He hesitated a moment, looking around the waiting area. "Well, it isn't as if I have anything pressing to do this afternoon."

"Yeah, what's up with that?" She too looked around. "I'd expect this place to be packed with patients since you're such a great vet. But maybe it is empty because *you are* a great vet and you keep your animals well."

"I'm flattered you think so, but my patient list isn't that long."

Jama frowned. "How do you normally get patients?"

He shrugged. "Word of mouth mostly. Why?"

"Perhaps you need to invest in a little advertising. Depending on your budget you could do a few radio ads, maybe a billboard or two around town. Get your name out there. Giveaways work great too. Setting up boxes in area businesses offering a free office visit or vaccination with visit can also drum up clientele."

"I'm listed in the phone book."

"Great. What about the Internet? Do you have a website?"

"No."

"You should consider one or at least buy advertising space on the Internet. What about a blog? You could write a weekly column on keeping your pet healthy. Have you considered participating in social media? Creating a page on a local site is a good tactic to get your name out there. Pet owners search the web for all kinds of reasons these days. A banner ad set to rotate with other advertisers would be a wise investment."

He grinned. "I thought you were taking the afternoon off."

"I am."

"It sounds like you're trying to sell me on an advertising campaign."

Jama swallowed. *He's right. I'm a freaking workaholic.* "Sorry. I didn't mean to go into sales mode."

"It's okay. I think you have good ideas and I sure could use the help getting more business. Sometimes I wonder if I'm in the wrong part of town."

"If you want, I'll do a feasibility study on the area and run the numbers to see where you stand. I'll also work up a full campaign plan with options and prices."

"Okay. I'd appreciate it." He stood, taking off his lab coat. He hung it on a hook behind the desk and pushed the stool back in place with his foot. "How does Italian sound for lunch?"

"Excellent."

"Let me send the phones to my service and we'll go."

"Where's Vikki?"

Kyle grinned as he dialed the phone. "She's probably floating on a cloud with a cowboy by now."

"What?"

"I'll explain it over lunch. Ready?"

"Sure."

Lunch at The Villa was a treat Kyle rarely enjoyed. First, because he worked during the day and second, because of the pricey menu. However, the delicious food made up for the expense, and he didn't want to take Jama anywhere too shabby. He especially liked dining on the patio because of its Italian village atmosphere and the instrumental music wafting from the sound system.

"This is wonderful," Jama said, opening up a menu. "I don't get out to this side of town often so I had no idea this place existed."

"Yeah. It's the South side's hidden surprise."

She scanned the entrée choices. "So tell me about Vikki."

Kyle chuckled and Jama put down her menu. "I had a cowboy show up with his ailing horse this morning. He walked the stallion right into the waiting area."

"He didn't!"

"Vikki flipped over him. She went so far as to remove her belly ring."

"She did?"

Kyle nodded.

"I never would have thought a cowboy was Vikki's type."

"Neither would I. Let's call her choice in clothes and men eclectic."

"What about her hair color? From what you've told me she changes it regularly."

"Yep. But today was different. She actually looked nice for a change; it was dark brown. I think that is her natural color, but it has been so long since I've seen it, I might be wrong. I just hope I did the right thing by having her accompany him to a local farm so the horse could get some fresh grass."

Jama reached across the table and placed her hand over his for a brief moment. "I'm sure she's fine."

"But is he?"

Jama opened her menu again and giggled as the waiter came to take their order.

During their meal, Kyle noticed a difference in her. She was more relaxed than he'd seen before. Being out of the office looked well on her, and he hoped she would consider taking time off more often. Spending it with him wouldn't be bad either.

"What are you staring at?" she asked, putting down her fork.

"You."

"Do I have a marinara smudge on my chin?" She reached for her napkin.

"No." He watched her fidget, amused at how quickly she became uncomfortable. The relaxed Jama was definitely different from the business woman. He found the switch from confident and secure to uncertain and shy downright adorable and unexpected.

"Then what?"

"Does there have to be a reason?"

"Of course. Unless—"

A silent pause lingered in the air. Their gazes locked. Kyle saw expectation mingled with doubt, piquing his interest further. "Unless?"

She looked away and shrugged. "You tell me."

He grinned. "You're a very interesting woman, Jama Wright."

"Interesting? I don't know about that. I had a co-worker point out today just how dull I am."

"Ouch."

"Tell me about it. But it's the truth. I'm a workaholic. I've forgotten how to step back and enjoy life."

"Then here's to turning over a new leaf." Kyle raised his iced tea glass.

She clinked hers with his. "I might need a little nudge now and then to keep me on the right path."

"Nudging will be enforced at your command."

"Thanks."

"So now that we've had our lunch, where should we go, Ms. Wright?"

She thought for a moment and then smiled. "I think we should go rescue that poor cowboy from Vikki."

Chapter Eight

Kyle bit back a smirk. "Okay, we'll go save him. However, I think we should take my Jeep; the road to the farm is a little rough in spots. Besides, it's a beautiful day and I've got the rag top off. Let's swing back by the clinic and get it."

"Sure." Jama picked up one of the chocolate covered mints the waiter left with the check. "I just love these."

Kyle grinned. "Puts a nice ending on an Italian meal, doesn't it?"

"Yes."

The short drive to the clinic took only minutes. Once Jama settled in the passenger seat of the Jeep and strapped on her seat belt, he pulled out of the parking lot.

When they stopped at a red light, he noticed from the corner of his eye that she tightly held onto the dash handgrip.

"Is my driving scaring you?"

"No. Why?"

"You're knuckles are turning white."

She frowned and released her hold. "Oh. I didn't even realize it. I was thinking about drumming up more awareness for your clinic."

He lightly punched her left arm and winked. "Nudge."

"What?"

"I'm giving you a nudge. You asked me to keep you on the right path. Today is a 'no work' day. Remember? Forget business. Tomorrow you can work."

"Yes, doctor." Her cheeks flushed and she tilted her head to the side, looking at him through thick lashes. "But my mind automatically wanders to thoughts of work. What can I do to change it?"

The light turned to green and he eased his foot off the clutch and accelerated with the traffic. "We need to recondition your thinking process."

"What?" she asked, the wind blowing her hair in her face as the vehicle picked up speed.

He raised his voice. "I said we need to recondition your thinking process."

"Oh."

At the next red light he asked. "Do you ever dream?"

"Everyone dreams. We might not always remember them when we wake up."

"I'm not talking about that kind of dreaming. Do you ever fantasize about what you want most?"

"You." Jama slapped her hand over her mouth as soon as the word slipped out. The gris-gris instantly burned her flesh, making the situation worse. She sneaked a glance at him and saw a smile at the corner of his mouth.

The light changed and he shifted gears. He didn't say anything more as he drove. He didn't even look her way. She swallowed hard praying they'd stop soon at another light and she could explain that she didn't mean it in the way it sounded. Well, she probably did, but she couldn't let him know that. At least not yet.

Instead, he slowed and turned off the two-lane road onto a dirt drive. About a hundred yards in he parked the Jeep in a small clearing. Undoing his seat belt, he turned to face her. "You want me?"

"Yes. I mean . . . I think about being with you. No. I mean spending time with you. You know, doing things together." She silently groaned at her babbling, knowing she was making it worse, but she had to explain herself. It just wasn't coming out right. Taking a deep breath she tried again. "I enjoy your company."

"That makes us even. I enjoy spending time with you too. In fact, I wasn't calling to check on Duke today. I called because I wanted to talk to you. I wanted to see you, but I wasn't sure if you felt the same."

"You did?"

He nodded.

"So when you called me honey at the hospital, it wasn't an accident?"

He shook his head.

"Oh." She shifted in the seat. "And the kiss?"

"Something I've wanted to do since I first laid eyes on you. But I wasn't certain how you'd react so I kept it light."

Her cheeks flamed. He liked her. She was thirty years old and blushing like a teenager. The butterflies she always felt when he was around danced in her stomach. Her mom used to call those symptoms of puppy love, but Jama had a suspicion her condition was way beyond that. She couldn't explain it, but ever since she met him she felt she was under a spell that she didn't mind being under.

The gris-gris burned hotter against her chest and a ray of light flashed from it. Startled, she frowned. Lucinda hadn't said anything about the gris-gris acting like this.

"Is that bad?"

Jama shook her head. "No. No it isn't," she assured him. "It's a little scary. I haven't had the best of luck with men. The last one tried to ruin my business."

"I'm sorry, honey." He reached out and touched her hand. Tiny tingles danced up her arm and warmth flittered through her stomach.

"No need to feel that way. It's over, and Wright & Associates is stronger than ever. I'm even taking my first vacation in over two years at the end of the summer."

"I'm glad to hear it." He squeezed her hand and she looked up, their gazes locked.

She wanted very much for him to kiss her. She even thought of kissing him if he didn't do it soon. But neither had a chance to make it happen.

Vikki appeared over the small hill astride a horse. She galloped toward them and stopped beside the Jeep. "Hey Kyle, what are you doing here? Hello, Ms. Wright. How's Duke?"

"He's fine."

"Where's Kit?" Kyle asked.

"Back at the barn fussing over Jasper. I swear he thinks more of that horse than himself, won't leave the animal's side."

"Cowboys normally do. Is the horse worse?"

Vikki shrugged. "Not that I can tell, but what do I know? You're the vet."

"Maybe I'd better have another look at him."

"Yeah. And tell Kit he has to give the horse space. We haven't even eaten lunch yet. I'm starving. Please, Kyle. Get him out of the barn for me."

"Okay. This once I'll do it."

"Great. You're the best. I'll race you back."

"I'm not racing you," Kyle said, but his words were unheard as Vikki turned the horse and galloped along the dirt path to the paddock. He started the engine and drove slowly along the rough drive.

"Sounds like Kit's held his own," Jama said loudly to be heard over the motor.

"Yeah. Unfortunately for Vikki."

He stopped the Jeep where the drive ended and after he got his bag out of the back, they walked over to the barn. A few chickens scattered as they approached. Two Billy goats butted heads in the lot, and from the open door of the barn he saw Vikki take the bridle off the horse.

Kyle walked over to the older man who appeared from the side of the barn. "Good afternoon, Hank."

"Hello, Kyle. I wasn't expecting to see you until in the morning."

"I know, but I got to thinking Vikki might be a handful."

The man gave a belly laugh. "She's been fine, but I know what you mean. She's stuck like glue to that young fella's side, though he hasn't seemed to notice much."

"That's what she said."

Hank looked over at Jama. "Who you got with you?"

Kyle motioned for her to join them. "Hank McDougal, this is Jama Wright."

"Nice to meet you, ma'am."

"Same here, Mr. McDougal. You have a lovely farm."

"It's home and we like it. Millie will insist you both stay for supper. Can I tell her to set a few more plates?"

Kyle looked at Jama and arched his brow. "What do you say? You don't have any plans for the evening, do you?"

"Only taking Duke for his jog." She smiled. "Thanks for the offer, Mr. McDougal. We'd be happy to stay."

"Hank, ma'am. Call me Hank." He beamed. "If you'll excuse me, I'll go tell Millie."

Kyle offered Jama his hand and they went into the barn. He saw Kit at the opposite end standing at the stall door, brushing Jasper. Vikki stood to his right, feeding the horse from the palm of her hand.

"They'd make a cute couple," Jama said. "And it's obvious from the change in her appearance and behavior after meeting him today, he'd be good for her too."

"That's what I was thinking, but he's only in town temporarily. I don't think my uncle would appreciate his little girl running off with a cowboy. He wouldn't think too kindly of me for encouraging her to get to know the boy either."

"Too bad there isn't a reason for him to stay," Jama mused as they walked toward the couple.

"I know."

Vikki turned and spotted them. "Kyle, Jasper's eating chopped carrots. Isn't that a good sign?"

"Sure is." He patted Kit on the back. "How does he seem to you?"

"He's much better." Kit turned and tipped his hat to Jama. "Howdy, ma'am."

"Hello."

Vikki stepped closer to Kit. "I was just telling him how we should take Jasper for a walk down to the creek for him to drink."

"Good idea. It's pure mountain water. And the walk through the pasture would be good for him."

"I suppose. I'm concerned about him though," Kit voiced.

"But the fresh air will be good for him," Vikki added. "And we can get out of this barn too."

Kit grinned down at her. "You've been a good sport, hanging around with me all afternoon."

"It's been my pleasure. So are we going or what?"

"We're going." He turned and tipped his hat again. "Dr. Landers. Ma'am."

"See you two later." Vikki practically giggled, hopping up on the stall door as it swung backwards. Kit walked the horse out and she jumped down, letting the door swing shut before falling into step alongside Jasper.

"Should we follow them?" Kyle asked.

"No."

"Why?"

"This is my day off, remember? I want to go exploring."

"Okay. Let's start up in the loft." He pointed to a ladder built between two stalls.

"What's up there?"

"Hay. Lots of hay."

"Why would I want to go up there to see it when there's a stack in the corner over there? What's so special about the hay up there?"

"Those are in bales. The hay up there is loose. Good for pitching into the stalls down below. It's also a great place to play."

"Really? I can't tell you the last time I frolicked."

"Then it's about time to change that."

Jama shook her head.

"No? What if I told you there's a momma cat with kittens up there."

"Hmmm. What kind?"

"Marmalade's an orange tabby. Hank thinks the papa of this litter is Old Blue because some of the kittens are orange and the others are grey."

"How many did she have?"

"Six. Four girls and two boys. Millie's picking out names."

Jama nodded. "What about the kittens at your clinic? Who do they belong to?"

"Esmeralda. Vikki's cat. She's trying to give them away, but so far no one has taken an interest. You want one?"

"No! You've seen how I am with Duke."

"I have. You're good with him. Sure it started out rough, but under the circumstances you did what any pet owner would do. You brought him to his vet."

She smiled. "Best move I could have made."

"You mean that?"

She nodded.

Kyle ran his hand up the back of her neck, pulling her closer to him. She stepped willingly into his embrace, and he kissed her deeply, exploring her mouth, the way he'd wanted for so long.

Chapter Nine

Hank cleared his throat. "Sorry for interrupting, but Millie's made lemonade. She's serving it up on the front porch."

The gris-gris burned warm against Jama's chest and she smiled. Perhaps Lucinda had been right about the charm. Maybe it did have magical powers that would bring her and her soul mate together.

"Lemonade would be great, Hank." Jama stepped slightly away from Kyle. She glanced up at him and his sheepish expression sent warm tingles soaring through her stomach.

She took his outstretched hand and they followed Hank up to the house.

Crossing a small foot bridge from the paddock to the front lawn, she spotted Millie pouring the drinks on the wrap around porch. The two-story farmhouse reminded her of the Walton's home from a TV program she watched as a girl. Except for the color. It had been a washed out white, whereas the McDougal's home was a pale-yellow with dark-green shutters. Also, the white split-rail railing that bordered the perimeter of the porch bowed out in the wedding cake fashion that was popular in the old south. On second thought the house wasn't anything like the Walton's but she got the feeling it held the same charm and warmth of a close knit family.

Jama didn't fancy herself an architectural buff, but she knew what she liked. She remembered wishing she lived in a house similar to this one growing up. Funny, she hadn't thought about that in years.

"Welcome," Mille greeted, wrapping Kyle in a motherly hug, which wasn't easy since she only came up to his chest. "It's so nice for you to visit without it being to make a house call." She didn't give him a chance to reply before she turned to Jama and did the same. "It's so good to have you here. Please have a seat."

"Thank you." Stunned by the greeting, Jama sat beside Kyle in the wicker swing.

Millie served the drinks and then sat beside Hank in the nearby wicker chairs, which engulfed her petite frame. She tucked her premature salt and pepper hair behind her ears and smiled at them. Clasping her hands together she broke the silence. "So are you dating?"

Hank chuckled. "Always subtle, dear."

"No point in beating around the bush. Especially when you know we want to know."

Kyle's face flushed red and a twinge of warmth flooded through Jama with expectation of his answer.

"Not exactly, but I'm hoping to change that." He looked at her as he stated his intentions.

She nodded and let out the breath she hadn't realized she held. The warmth of the gris-gris spiked a notch or two and she reached for the chain, playing with it.

"Wonderful." Millie beamed like a proud momma hen. "It's about time you found someone, Kyle."

He shifted in the seat and leaned close to Jama's ear. "Millie's been like a second mom since I came to town, fussing over and feeding me."

"Oh, I see."

"Do you work, Jama?"

"Yes. I'm in advertising."

"She's not just in advertising. She owns her own agency," Kyle added.

Jama heard the note of pride in his voice and it pleased her.

"Really?" Millie gave a playful smile. "You want children?"

"Millie," Hank scolded.

"I'm only asking what we're both wondering."

Kyle shifted in the swing again, his leg brushing against Jama's. Her cheeks flushed warm, all too aware of his closeness. But the question made her tense. Children? Did Millie know her mother? Now that Darren had married, their mother had at least shifted gears to focus on him and Keely producing the first grandchild. That took some pressure off of her, being the oldest, for the moment. And she didn't even want to give thought to her biological clock ticking in fast motion. In all honesty she didn't know if she wanted children. Her experience with Duke made her doubt her ability to raise a child.

"I haven't given that much thought," she said when Kyle remained silent. "My main focus has been on my business since college. And before you ask, the answer is no. I've never been married."

Hank cleared his throat and smiled. "She got you there, Millie."

His wife swatted at him with her hand. "Oh hush."

A pause fell over them and they all sipped their lemonade.

"How's your vegetable garden doing, Millie?" Kyle asked, changing the conversation to a safer subject.

"Excellent. In fact, everything we're having for supper is out of the garden."

"Even the chicken," Hank added.

"Yes. That hen won't be pecking at my tomatoes anymore."

Jama drained the lemonade from her glass and pushed the thought of Millie killing their dinner that morning out of her mind. It didn't set well with her. It made her feel a little ill thinking of feathers flying and Millie wielding a vengeful hatchet on the unsuspecting bird.

"You okay, Jama?" Kyle asked. "You're awfully quiet."

"Just thinking."

"About the clinic? Or about an ad campaign? Do you need another nudge?"

"Actually, neither. I was thinking about that chicken."

Millie, Hank and Kyle chuckled.

"You're not a vegetarian are you, dear?" Millie asked.

"No, ma'am.

"An animal rights activist?"

"No."

"I can assure you that chicken would have ended up on our dinner table one way or another." Millie stood and reached for the lemonade pitcher. "Oh there comes Vikki and that young man. Hank, go inside and get two more glasses."

"Yes dear."

"Mind if we join you?" Vikki asked.

"Of course not," Millie said. "Come sit on the settee. I believe there's enough room for both of you. Hank will be right back with more glasses."

"Thank you, ma'am." Kit tipped his hat then placed it on Vikki's head.

She turned to her cousin. "What do you think, Kyle? Would I make a good cowgirl?"

"Don't ask me. I'm not an expert on that."

"What do you think, Kit?" Vikki turned, tilted her head back and batted her lashes at him.

"Well, there's a lot more to being a cowgirl than just wearing a hat and sporting a pair of boots. I'd be glad to teach you if you were serious and I had the time. But it looks like I'll be moving on tomorrow, now that Jasper's feeling better."

Vikki's countenance fell as she put the hat back on his head. "That's okay. It was a nice thought anyway."

Hank reappeared and Millie poured more lemonade.

"I had a great idea earlier that might just make Vikki very happy," Jama announced.

Vikki's brows arched. "What's that?"

Jama smiled. "Kit, have you ever thought of doing a little acting?"

"Acting? No, ma'am, I haven't."

"Would you consider it?"

He shrugged.

"What are you getting at, Jama?" Kyle asked.

"I've been trying to come up with a good angle for an ad campaign for the Eastland Animal Clinic. Kyle's too good of a vet for him not to have more patients than he does."

"Yeah." Vikki chimed. "I've thought that too."

"Kit, Kyle told me you were on a rodeo circuit that raises money for charities."

"Yeah, but if I had the money I'd be doing it professionally."

"I was hoping you'd say that. Kyle needs to get his clinic's name out before the public. He could sponsor you by providing a horse trailer with his clinic's name on it. In return, you'd do a few commercials, television and radio spots, talking about the care Jasper was given at his clinic. I'll also line up a few other clients that would be willing to invest money for a little advertising in return. How does that sound to you?"

"I'd say that sounds like a great idea, ma'am."

"What do you think, Kyle?"

Kyle grinned and rubbed his hand up and down the back of his head. "It's worth a shot."

"Is that a yes?" Vikki asked.

"It's a yes." Kyle nodded.

"All right!" Vikki cheered. "What can I do?"

"Your job will be to provide excellent customer service to pet owners that call in to make appointments," Jama said.

"Don't I already do that?" Vikki frowned.

"Yes." Jama smiled. "When I called about Duke you gave me invaluable advice about staying calm so I wouldn't cause him more distress. It's little details like that, that make a difference."

Kyle got up from the swing and draped an arm around his cousin's shoulders. "But you'll need to lose the gum popping. And no more watching your stories in the afternoons."

"Oh." Vikki bit her lower lip then smiled. "I can do it."

"This sounds exciting," Millie chimed.

"It will be," Jama said.

Chapter Ten

Jama went to bed that night with a smile on her face. After having dinner with the McDougals, Kyle had followed her home so she could change clothes. Then they both took Duke for his daily jog. Afterward they walked a few laps around the Fountain City duck pond holding hands and talking over ideas for the advertising campaign she'd be launching for him. The only downside had been when he brought her home and they had to say goodnight. It had been hard to let him go. His kiss goodbye had left her breathless, and she was still feeling its effects as she slipped under the covers, alone.

She was dreaming of being with him on a catamaran in the blue waters of the Caribbean when a shrill noise woke her. Fumbling to turn on the bedside lamp, she knocked off the picture frame of Darren and Duke. The crack of the glass as it hit the hardwood floor made her wince. "Great," she grumbled, grabbing the cordless phone.

"Hello?"

"Finally. This is Mr. Brubaker from next door. Can't you hear that dog of yours? If you don't shut him up I'm calling Animal Control."

"What?" Jama pulled the phone away from her ear and listened. Sure enough she heard the mournful howl of Duke. It had been a few nights since he'd done this. Why had she thought the dog was over his affliction? Silently groaning she placed the phone back to her ear. "I'm sorry Mr. Brubaker. I must have been sound asleep. I'll take care of him. I'm sorry he disturbed you."

"It isn't like this is the first time. There are laws against this kind of public disturbance. I have my rights."

"I'm aware of those, sir. Like I said I'll take care of it. I'm sorry he disturbed you. Good night."

Jama hung up and counted to five, before she called Kyle.

"Hello?" His sleep filled voice came over the receiver.

"Sorry to wake you, but it's Duke. He's howling again. He woke up the neighbor. I'm on my way down to check on him. I thought I'd better call. I'm sure he's fine, but…"

"Okay. I'll be there in a few."

"Thank you." She hung up and carefully got out of bed to avoid the broken glass of the picture frame. Cleaning up the fragments in haste, she set the frame on the dresser before she hurried to slip into a pair of jeans and a t-shirt. Once outside she found Duke lying on the ground under the moon, moaning.

"This has got to stop, boy." She knelt beside him and rubbed his side. "You have to stop waking up the neighbors."

Duke whimpered.

"We can't be doing this every night until Darren and Keely return. They are coming back, you know. And once they do you'll see you're missing them like this was for nothing."

"Wooolf."

"Yes. You haven't been abandoned. They've only gone on a short trip. They'll be back. Once they return you'll be rid of me. You won't have to see me every day. Only when they invite me over. If they invite me over."

Duke wagged his tail and licked at her hand.

The flickering of headlights announced Kyle's arrival as the Jeep pulled into the drive. He cut the motor and the lights before he walked over to where Jama knelt beside the dog.

"What seems to be the problem tonight?"

"I'm not sure. He was howling pretty loudly until I came out. He settled down to a whimper before his moaning subsided. I did feel tightening in his abdomen when I was rubbing him."

"You did?"

Jama nodded.

He felt of his stomach. "Nothing unusual there. Maybe he was gassed."

"This is getting old. The neighbors have been nice up until now about Duke's howling, but Mr. Brubaker threatened to call Animal Control if I couldn't keep him quiet."

"Mr. Brubaker is a crotchety old man. I've heard a few unpleasant tales about him from your other neighbors concerning their cats."

"He doesn't sound like a nice person."

Kyle shook his head and was silent for a moment. "The night I stayed over Duke had no problem sleeping on the back porch. He quieted down and slept all night. Let's try him there again tonight. Keely and Darren didn't say anything about that being where he normally sleeps, did they?"

"No they didn't." Jama thought back to the list of instructions Darren had gone over with her, but was sure he hadn't mentioned the dog sleeping on the porch. "If that is what this has all been about…I'll clobber Darren for not telling me. The tests. The exams. The sleep-interrupted nights."

"Save your anger, honey. It's only a thought and a possible solution." Kyle reached for her hand. "I haven't minded the sleep-interrupted nights. Have you?"

Jama looked at him and shook her head, getting to her feet with his help. "No. I can't say I have."

He pulled her into his arms, holding her close. "I'm glad you had to call me tonight. I wasn't sleeping too well anyway. I couldn't get our goodnight kiss out of my head."

"You couldn't?"

"No."

"I was dreaming." She breathed in the smell of him and the tension she'd felt earlier melted away.

"Anything good?"

"Extremely." She wrapped her arms around him and smiled. He tilted his head toward hers and they kissed. Her pulse quickened and she felt the gris-gris begin to burn against her skin.

Kyle broke their kiss and pulled away. He glanced down and frowned. "Jama, did you know that necklace you are always wearing is glowing? And I swear I felt it grow hot while we kissed."

She took a deep breath and nodded. Would he believe her if she told him the charm was supposed to possess powers? She hadn't really wanted to believe it herself, but it did some of the strangest things while she wore it. "I know."

His frown deepened. "Don't you find that odd?"

She slipped her arm through his and they walked toward the porch, Duke followed them. "Yes. Very odd. But this necklace is special. It was given to me by Keely, who received it from a family friend. It is supposed to bring me good luck."

"Really?"

That was the first time since they met that she heard skepticism in his voice. "It is supposed to have brought Keely and my brother Darren together. Some might say it brought us together too."

"And here I thought Duke had brought us together." Kyle chuckled, reaching for the screened porch door. He opened it and Duke went in ahead of them, settling on the rug. "Maybe that is his spot after all."

Jama studied the dog in the moonlight. He did look content curled up there. "I wish I had known."

Without a word, Kyle cupped her face in his hands and kissed her again. Warmth flowed through her body and she leaned into him, never wanting the kiss to end. But it did all too quickly. She saw longing in his eyes and he took a ragged breath before he spoke.

"I better head home. The sun will be coming up before we know it."

She nodded, wishing she had the nerve to ask him to stay, even if they only snuggled on the couch, but this wasn't her house. And she wasn't sure she was ready to jump into anything more with him. Wasn't it only a few hours ago that they'd confessed they had feelings for one another? The way she felt at the moment it seemed much longer, but was this possibly the effects of the gris-gris or a spell she was under?

"Jama? Is something wrong?"

His question brought her out of her thoughts. "No. I was wishing you didn't have to go, but I have a big presentation tomorrow."

"And a new campaign to put together." His reminder made her smile.

"I won't forget that. I'll call you when I have some figures put together and we'll see where you want to go with the campaign."

"That sounds like a plan." He caressed her cheek with his hand, slowly running his fingers along her jawline, breaking the caress. "Call me if our patient needs me."

"I will. Thanks for coming over."

"Thanks for calling me."

She smiled and when he'd slipped out the door, she fastened the latch. He ran to his jeep and started the motor. Backing up, he turned before he pulled out of the drive onto the road. She finally turned toward the dog and saw he'd already fallen asleep so she quietly went back into the house, locking the door behind her.

The ringing phone woke Jama for the second time. She pushed herself up in bed and reached for the phone. "Hello?"

"Ms. Wright, it's Pamela. Are you okay?"

"I was sleeping." Her eyes opened fully, noticing the tiny ray of light peeking through the curtains, and she realized her secretary never called her at home unless there was an emergency. "Pamela, why are you calling me in the middle of the night?"

The brief silence on the line was awkward. "It isn't the middle of night, Ms. Wright. Don't you know what time it is?"

She turned in bed and reached for her watch. The big hand was on the six and the little hand was a little past the nine. The second hand pulsated slowly, yet she feared her watch had somehow stopped working. She smacked it against the palm of her hand trying to change the reading, but that didn't work. To her dismay, she had to admit she was late for work.

"Did you oversleep?"

She silently groaned. This was not happening to her. She took one day off, slightly changing her routine, and the next day everything began to fall apart. She'd even left her briefcase in her office when she rushed out yesterday. Thinking back to the night before when she'd crawled into bed thinking about Kyle, she didn't recall setting the alarm. She'd been distracted. Something she rarely allowed to happen.

"Are you still there, Ms. Wright?" Pamela's question reminded her that her assistant expected an explanation.

"Yes. I'm here. I must have forgotten to set the alarm. Quick, what time is my presentation with Kernell?"

"Eleven forty-five at their west office. Relax. You have time to get there."

Jama thought for a second as she got out of bed. There was not enough time for her to get ready, go to the office and then go clear across town. "Pamela, I'll need you to gather my presentation materials, get my briefcase and appointment book from my office, and meet me there at eleven thirty."

"Certainly. Anything else?"

"Not a word of this to anyone in the office. Is that clear? I've never overslept in my life or been late to work. I don't know what has come over me."

"You can count on me."

"Good. See you then."

Hanging up the phone, she rushed to the bathroom to get ready. As she pulled off her nightgown, the gris-gris got caught in the fabric, and she had to slow down to keep from choking herself. "Great. Just what I need, more complications."

For a brief moment she contemplated removing the charm. But Lucinda's warning not to take it off made her think twice. Her day had already started off badly. She didn't want to tempt fate with a reason to make it worse. Nor did she want to give fate a reason to end what had begun between her and Kyle.

Chapter Eleven

Jama was never so happy to pull in the driveway as she was at half-past five that evening. She went inside and changed into her running outfit before cajoling Duke into the backseat of her car. Taking the dog for his run sounded heavenly after the day she'd had. Her meeting with Kernell Glassware had been going fine until she'd agreed to a late lunch with the CEO. They'd run into a former client of Ted Donaldson's, and the man had not been pleasant about his experience with her agency, all because of Ted. It had been two years already. When would she be rid of him and the stigma he'd left on her business? Luckily she'd been able to think fast on her feet and keep the CEO of Kernell from reconsidering their agreement and his sponsorship for Kit Blakenship.

She'd had little time to begin work on the feasibility report for Kyle, but hopefully she'd have time tonight to run a few figures. Parking at the Fountain City Lake, she got out and opened the back door, snapped on Duke's leash and headed toward the trail. She'd never been a jogger, but she was able to keep a good pace that Duke seemed to enjoy. And she didn't mind stopping when he got distracted by the squirrels or the ducks or a stray butterfly that flitted into his path.

As they finished their last lap she saw Kyle standing by his jeep in the small parking area. Duke noticed him too and took off at a full run, practically dragging her until her feet caught up with him. "Slow down, boy," she called.

Kyle waved. "Hi."

"Hi, yourself." She pulled the dog's leash tighter to keep a good hold on him. "What brings you out this way?"

"I had to make a house call for one of my elderly clients at the assisted living facility not far from here. I was passing by when I spotted you and Duke. So I thought I'd stop and see how things are going."

She smiled. "Then it's our lucky day. Isn't that right, boy?"

Glancing down, she saw Duke had flopped down on the ground at Kyle's feet and it looked like he was snoozing. However, his tail wagged a few times, acknowledging he'd been spoken to.

"He's really glad to see you," she assured Kyle.

"I know." He stooped down and patted the dog on the head. "Did you bring any water for him?"

She snapped her fingers. "I knew I was forgetting something today. When I got home all I had on my mind was getting here so I could return and take care of some unfinished business."

"I thought you were going to take some time for yourself?" Kyle looked up at her. "You know, work on being less of a workaholic."

"I am…I will, but today started off bad and didn't get any better. Plus I promised I'd run those figures for you and I don't want to keep you waiting."

He stood and reached for her hand, giving it a squeeze. "Those figures can wait. My business, while not the best it could be, has been holding its own for some time now. Sure, I'd like to see it pick up, but don't stress yourself on my account. My campaign doesn't have to be top priority."

"Thank you, but it's that reason I want to work on it. You're too good of a vet for others not to know it. We need to spread the word."

"They will. In time."

Duke yawned and shook his head. His jaws shook and a high-pitched noise escaped him. They both looked down as the dog got to his feet.

"I think he's ready to go now. Do you want to come by for dinner?"

Kyle laughed.

"I have fresh vegetables for a salad?"

"I'll pass, but thanks."

She shook her head. "You're not going to forget the Hunan incident are you?"

"Not yet. But thanks for the offer. I'm headed to the McDougals. They've invited me to dinner again. Millie said I should bring you too. How about it?"

"I wish I could, but taking yesterday off has put me behind. I need to play catch up tonight or I'll be working all weekend instead of a few hours Saturday morning. Maybe next time?" She tilted her head to the side and smiled. "Tell Millie I'm sorry."

He nodded. "Okay. As long as you promise you'll try to make it the next time."

"I do, Kyle."

He stepped closer and pulled her to him, brushing his lips against hers. "I'll hold you to it, Ms. Wright."

"Woooolf." Duke jumped up, putting his paws on Kyle's leg, nudging his head between them.

He rubbed the dog's head. "I think he's in agreement."

She laughed.

"All it takes is a few baby steps, Jama. Take baby steps and you'll modify your life."

She stepped backwards and jerked the dog's leash, causing him to jump down and follow her. "I'll see you later."

Kyle nodded. "See you."

The next morning, Jama studied the storyboard layout on her desk and stood. There was something not right about the sequence, but she couldn't put her finger on it. Taking her cup, she walked over to her credenza and the carafe of hot coffee to pour herself more.

Light tapping drew her attention to her open doorway. "Are you busy?" Judith asked.

An uneasy feeling crept over her at the sight of her business manager. Rarely did Judith pop in to see her, especially twice in one week. "Not sure. Depends on whether you have good news for me or not."

Judith laughed. "Our financials are great. Couldn't be better right now."

"Then why did my insides knot up at the sight of you?"

"Foreshadowing?"

Jama grimaced. "I don't like it when you talk like that. Come in and shut the door. Do you want some coffee?"

"I'm good. And it really isn't that bad. I do think you should have a seat though."

Jama waited until Judith was seated before she joined her on the loveseat. She took a long sip of her coffee, set the cup down on the accent table in front of them and inhaled deeply, before she slowly let out the breath. "Okay. I can take it."

"You really are getting worked up over nothing," Judith assured. "I'm curious, have you ever thought of selling Wright & Associates?"

"What?"

"You heard me. Have you ever considered it?"

Jama shook her head. "No. Not even when we were scraping rock bottom after Ted…That was the last thing I wanted to have happen."

"I didn't think so and I told Lynch that."

"Lynch? You've been talking to Ferguson Lynch?"

Judith nodded. "He cornered me at a reception I went to last night. He said there is a New York firm looking to branch out in the south and he felt Wright & Associates would be the perfect agency to pitch. If you were interested."

"*If* I'm interested, which I'm not. Why'd he seek you out? Why didn't he come straight to me?"

"I think he felt he could test the waters with me before he even attempted to contact you. I had to promise to pass along the proposition before he'd let me leave the event." Judith reached into her jacket pocket and pulled out a business card. "He said to call him if you want to discuss it."

Jama took the card and stared at it for a moment. "We're finally on our feet. Do we even need the backing of a New York agency?"

"Only you can decide that." Judith got to her feet. "Are you willing to give up control of your company?"

"I don't want to. It's my baby."

"Then maybe that's your answer, but if you think there could ever be a time when we'll be vulnerable again, when another Ted Donaldson could weasel his way in…wouldn't it be nice to have security?"

Jama shook her head. She'd never allow another Ted Donaldson into her life. But she was allowing Kyle into it. He wasn't as dangerous as Ted. He only wanted her to work less, to relax more. If what Lynch said was true, making a deal with a New York firm could free her up. Give her the time to be more carefree. Was that freedom worth the cost?

"Thanks, Judith. I have a lot to think about. If Lynch should contact you again to follow up, you can tell him I'm considering the possibilities."

"I'm not saying I'm for this, Jama. I wouldn't want you to think I'm pushing you toward it. I'm only delivering the message."

"I know." Jama stood. "I think I'll give Darren a call. I hate to bother him on his honeymoon, but who better to advise me on New York than him? Lynch didn't happen to mention the name of the company looking to branch out?"

Judith shook her head. "I'm afraid not."

"Okay. Thanks."

"No problem. If you need anything…numbers, financials for the last six weeks, months, or year let me know and I'll be happy to run a new set of reports for you."

"I'll let you know."

After Judith left, Jama refilled her coffee cup and went back to her desk. Glancing down at the storyboards she saw the problem clearly this time, marked it with a sticky flag and buzzed her secretary.

"Pamela, I need these boards returned to production for correction."

"Yes, Ms. Wright. I'll be right there."

She sat down in her chair and debated whether she should give Ferguson Lynch a call to find out what he knew about the New York agency before she called Darren. She knew her brother would be able to advise her better that way, but did she risk sending the wrong signal to Lynch? She didn't want word to spread around town that Wright & Associates was open to a merger before she even made a decision.

Several minutes later Pamela entered her office with a package wrapped in brown paper. "Sorry to take so long, but this just arrived for you by messenger."

Jama took the box. "It's kinda heavy."

"I know. The man said he was instructed to be very careful with it because it contained breakable material."

"There's no return address."

"I noticed that too, but the delivery guy was one we've used before so I wasn't concerned that the package could contain explosives or anything."

Jama looked up at her quickly, making a face. "Gee thanks for that notion, Pamela."

Her secretary shrugged. "You never know these days what some crazy nut might do. Anyway, I was wondering if Kernell might have sent you samples of their glassware."

That was a thought and it made her relax a little. "I guess there is only one way to find out." Jama set the package on her desk. She picked up her letter opener and slipped it underneath the folds to cut the tape before she removed the paper wrapping to find a black square box trimmed in gold etching. Removing the lid, she saw the inside was covered with black felt and cushioned within its folds was a crystal orb held by a brushed antique golden base.

"That's gorgeous. But who sent it?" Pamela asked.

Jama pulled it out of the box and set it on her desk. "I don't know. There isn't a card."

"Wait, there's something," Pamela pointed to a small lavender colored card at the bottom of the box. She picked it up and handed it to her.

"To bring you clarity when you need it —Lucinda," Jama read aloud.

"Who's Lucinda?"

"A friend of Keely's." Jama stared at the inscription on the piece of paper wondering how Lucinda knew what she was going through at that very moment. Glancing at the crystal orb, she also wondered what that was supposed to do for her. If she peered into it would she see her future?

Reaching up to her neck, she fingered the gris-gris. If she bought into the magic of it, then shouldn't she also buy into the orb? Nah. That would be ridiculous. Wouldn't it?

"That is gorgeous and so very interesting," Pamela said, reaching to pick up the orb. She turned it as she looked at it. "Oh, would you look at that."

"What?" Jama stood.

"It's one of those musical things. Like snow globes, except this isn't one. See the little crank."

Jama inspected it with her and then turned the little crank. A tune began to play and she looked up at her secretary and they both said, *"Some Enchanted Evening."*

"I need to meet this, Lucinda. She gives the best gifts." Pamela handed Jama the orb and picked up the storyboards. "I'll take these to production."

Jama nodded and turned the crank to wind it again, letting the music play. She smiled, thinking about Kyle and the first night they met. It was an evening she'd never forget. Was that what Lucinda was trying to tell her? That Kyle wasn't the problem she needed to fix?

Chapter Twelve

"OMG!" Vikki exclaimed staring at an oversized postcard that came in the day's mail. "OMG!"

"What is it?" Kyle asked, leaning over to the counter.

Vikki glanced up from the card and shook her head. "You're never going to believe this."

"I don't know if I will until I find out what you're going on about."

"Here." She shoved the card at him. "Take a long hard look at those knockers and tell me you don't recognize her."

Kyle blinked and looked closely at the scantily clad showgirl on the card. He swallowed, feeling a tightening in his throat and an even tighter knot in his stomach. Carol.

"I can't believe that B—"

"Vikki," he cut her off and turned the card over. It was addressed to him in Carol's perfect script with a note that she'd like to see him while she was in town. It appeared she was on tour with a dance troop out of Vegas. At least her dream of being a showgirl was coming true.

"Tell me you aren't going to see her."

Vikki's statement cut into his thoughts. He shrugged. "I don't know."

"What about Jama? Or did seeing the B on the card make you forget all about her?"

Kyle grimaced at Vikki's tone. He'd never heard her talk so negative about a person before. "I haven't forgotten her. We don't know what Carol wants to see me about. Maybe she's grown and wants to apologize for her past behavior."

Vikki laughed. "You been watching Oprah or Dr. Phil again? Cause only they'd be spouting off that stuff."

"Don't you have some filing to do?" he asked.

She glared at him. "Fine. Brush me aside, but if you see Carol and she deflates your ego, don't come running to me whining cause I don't want to hear it. All you'll get from me is the hand and the hand doesn't want to hear it either."

"Vikki."

"I'm going. Don't get all huffy with me." She handed him the rest of the unopened mail and went through the doorway to the adjacent room where they kept the patients files.

When she was gone, he went around the counter and settled in the chair, wondering if he dared see Carol when she came to town. He really had no desire to see her, but now that Vikki had made such a stink telling him he shouldn't, it made him want to prove his young cousin wrong. But he knew she was right. Seeing Carol was not going to change anything. The woman was bad news and his life had changed for the better when she walked out of it.

Besides he had Jama in his life now. And they were doing all right. She was more of a workaholic than he liked, but she had already made a few modifications to change that. He liked the fact that Jama had approached the subject instead of him. Not that he would have. He would have accepted her for who she was just like she would have to accept him for who he is.

The phone rang and he answered it, scheduling an appointment for a new patient that afternoon. Yes. This was good. Word of mouth brought him at least one if not two new patients a month. Maybe he really didn't need the advertising campaign Jama was putting together for him. If he became too busy he'd have less time to spend with her and growing their relationship. At least he hoped what they had was turning into a relationship.

He hadn't spent time like this with another woman since Carol. He'd been content taking care of his patients, fighting on a regular basis with Vikki, and having the occasional meal with the McDougals. Meeting Jama was changing all of that for him and he felt he was ready for it. But was she? They'd hardly seen each other now that Duke had stopped having his nightly symptoms. He didn't wish ill on the dog, but another flare up couldn't hurt. That seemed to be the only way Jama stopped focusing on her business and paid attention to the world around her.

Was he willing to play second fiddle to her work? She promised to slow down, to stop working so much, but could a workaholic do it? Even when she wasn't working, her mind went back to it. He'd seen that firsthand the day she decided he needed an advertising campaign. That proved she was her own worst enemy and he was determined to see she break the vicious cycle before it was too late.

He reached for the phone and punched in Jama's number. He listened as it rang once, twice, three times. Finally a female voice came on the line, but it wasn't Jama.

"Wright & Associates. How can I direct your call?"

"Jama Wright please."

"I'm sorry. Ms. Wright is on another line at the moment. Can I take a message and have her call you back?"

"Sure. Tell her Kyle Landers called. She has my number."

"Certainly, Mr. Landers. Have a nice day."

He hung up the phone disappointed that he hadn't gotten to speak to her, but it was during normal business hours so he couldn't fault her for working. Maybe she'd call him right back.

"Darren, I'm so glad you're having a great time on your honeymoon. You know I wouldn't have called if it wasn't important. I need your advice, little brother."

"You know I'm always here for you, Jama. What's this about?"

"Ferguson Lynch contacted Judith with the possibility of a New York firm wanting to branch out in the south. He thinks Wright & Associates would be a good fit. I've been giving this some thought and I'm not sure I want to move in that direction, but an opportunity like this doesn't come along every day either. What should I do?"

She heard a low whistle come through the phone. "That's a toughie. Having worked in New York I know what kind of cut-throat environment it can be, but so are the smaller markets if you examine them closely. You have to ask yourself if you are willing to take the necessary measures to keep the big dog happy at all costs. Wright &

Associates wouldn't be yours anymore. Sure, they'd probably let you keep the name, but the firm I was with acquired a few smaller ones during the time I was there and the outcome wasn't always pretty."

"I was almost afraid of that. So I shouldn't take a meeting with Lynch?"

"I didn't say that. It never hurts to know all of your options while you are making your final decision. Set something up. See what Lynch has to say, but make it clear to him you aren't sold on the idea. Once you do that call me back and we'll discuss it further. If Keely and I need to cut a few days off our trip we'll do it."

"No. No, don't cut your trip short. There's no need for that. I handled the Duke situation without bothering you. Don't make me regret calling you over this."

"The Duke situation? What's been going on with him?"

Jama winced at the slip of her tongue. She heard the alarm in Darren's voice and she also heard Keely in the background demanding to know what was going on with Duke. She had no choice but to tell him everything. "It turned out to be nothing. I called the vet and he checked the dog over. He's physically fine, but he was temporarily suffering from separation anxiety which caused him to howl at the moon and wake the neighbors. I never felt more inept in my life."

Darren laughed. "Are you serious? The dog was suffering from separation anxiety? Is that even possible?"

"It's possible and he ate up the attention he got while we figured it out. I had to rearrange my schedule, cancel meetings to take him to the vet. But Kyle has been great. He made house call after house call in the middle of the night. He even slept on the couch to make sure Duke didn't have another episode."

"Kyle? He's the vet? You let him sleep on the couch? But you hardly know him. Do you think that was wise?"

Jama frowned. She was a grown woman who could take care of herself. Where did her brother get off questioning her actions?

"Let me talk to her." Keely's voice came over the line louder than she had heard before mingled with scuffling over the receiver. "Hi Jama. I only got bits of what you were telling Darren. Duke is okay?"

"Yes. Kyle thought it was bloat at first. He ran a battery of tests and they all came back negative. Don't worry. I'll take care of the bill since he was in my care. Without any other explanation, it became clear that because Duke had changed ownership twice already that he felt he was being abandoned."

"How strange, but I can see that. Alex left him, but Duke at least knew me from where I took care of him before when my brother had to be out of town for short-term assignments. He hardly knew you at all. I'm so sorry you've had to go through this. We should have prepared you both better by letting you spend time together."

"It's not been that horrible." Jama thought about Kyle and knew she wouldn't have changed any of it because she might not have met him otherwise. "Duke's doing much better now that he's sleeping on the back porch. I hope that is okay?"

"Of course it's okay. That's where he sleeps. Didn't Darren tell you?"

Jama gritted her teeth. "No. My idiot brother didn't tell me."

"Sorry for the trouble. I hope everything else is going okay?"

"Everything's fine. You can tell Darren he owes me two weeks of vacation to make up for my trouble"

Keely giggled. "I'll tell him. How's the gris-gris? Have you met someone?"

"You could say that."

"Anyone I know?"

"Maybe."

Keely laughed. "Okay. Fair enough. Good for you. I'll get the details when I return. I have to get off now because Darren wants back on the line."

"Okay."

"So what do you know about this vet?" Darren asked.

"Enough to know he's good at what he does. Why don't you ask your wife? He was her vet before I started looking after Duke. I'll schedule a meeting with Lynch, and if I need to call you back before you get home, I will."

"You'd better," Darren warned. "If I don't hear from you I'll be calling."

Jama looked up and motioned at the doorway for Sue Charles to come on in. "All right. I need to go now. There's someone waiting to see me."

"Bye."

"Bye." She hung up the phone and took a deep breath. "Perfect timing."

Sue giggled. "A chatty client?"

"No. Darren. I called and then he had the nerve to start lecturing me on men."

Sue laughed, looking around the room. "Just like a protective sibling. Pamela said you had received a present today that I just had to see. I assumed it was flowers from your vet."

"No. Kyle didn't send me anything. Lucinda did. You remember Lucinda from the wedding don't you?"

"Yes. Lovely woman, but a little eccentric."

"She's more than a little eccentric." Without thinking, Jama reached up and touched the gris-gris.

Sue gasped. "Hey, you're wearing Keely's charm. She told me Lucinda gave it to her. Is that what you got?"

Jama shook her head and went over to the bookshelf where she'd put the crystal orb so it wouldn't get broken on her desk. "No. Lucinda sent me this. It's a lovely little music wind up piece."

"Oh. I see what Pamela meant by it being so breathtaking, but I had thought she meant the flowers were potent in fragrance."

Jama wound the little crank and let the music play. "Nice, don't you think?"

"Very. So tell me, if Lucinda didn't give you the gris-gris, then who did?"

"Keely, but Lucinda delivered it to me right after they left on their honeymoon."

"Did she do an incantation and all of that?" Sue asked.

Jama's brow arched. "How did you know about that?"

"Keely inadvertently told me. She was talking to herself one day while she worked, and she must have hit the intercom on the phone because it buzzed me and I heard her mumbling about Lucinda and the necklace and the incantation. She wasn't buying into it. That was during the time she and Darren were not talking because she found out he'd lied to her by not telling her he was Darren Wright of Wright & Associates."

Jama nodded. "So what do you think about the necklace holding powers and all that?"

Sue shrugged. "I'm all for good luck. And right now I could use some. I haven't been on a date in more months than I care to remember. Sometimes being single sucks."

Jama couldn't agree more. It was even harder sometimes to be single when you were seeing someone. But she couldn't say she was ready to take the next step yet either. And when she thought about it, she hadn't been seeing Kyle long enough to want more, yet she did. She wanted the happy ever after with him and that realization scared her. Was she really ready to give her heart away that easy?

Chapter Thirteen

Vikki walked into the waiting area, carrying Oswald on her arm. She opened the door and put him back in the cage. She glanced at Kyle sitting at her desk and planted her hands on her hips. "Why so glum, chum?"

"Kyle not with pretty lady. Kyle not with pretty lady," the bird squawked, ruffled his feathers and clung to the side of the cage.

Kyle glared at the cage, wadded up a piece of paper and threw it at the bird. "Shut up, why don't you."

Oswald squawked and fluttered to the other side of the cage.

"What's eating at you?" She frowned. "Did you talk to Carol?"

"No. I haven't talked to Carol."

"You told Jama about Carol, and she got upset?"

He shook his head. "Why would Jama get upset? I haven't seen Carol. I haven't spoken to her."

She shrugged. "Then what's wrong?"

"Nothing."

"I don't believe you."

"I'm fine. Jama's fine. At least I think she is."

Vikki snapped her fingers. "That's it. You haven't seen or talked to Jama in days now."

He didn't answer.

"That is it." She grabbed the broom and swept underneath the waiting room chairs without being asked. When she finished she turned and stared at him. "Why haven't you talked to her?"

"She hasn't returned my call. I left a message."

Vikki rolled her eyes. "Then call her, silly. I swear, Kyle. You don't think like an adult sometimes."

"Jama is a very busy business woman."

"Who would leap for joy to hear from you no matter how busy she may be. What if she didn't get your message? What if she thinks you're avoiding her? Maybe she's sitting in her office wondering why she hasn't heard from you."

Vikki had a point, but he didn't want her to know it. He got up from the desk and went over to the magazine rack. "How's Kip?"

"He's fine and Jasper too. He called me last night from Wacco. Don't change the subject. Are you going to call Jama or not?"

"I'll call her if you'll get off my back about it."

She winked at him. "Not another peep will you hear."

He headed to his office where he could have a little privacy. Closing the door behind him, he settled in his desk chair and called Jama's number.

Jama gathered up her presentation materials and slipped them into her briefcase. "I'll be out of the office for the rest of the afternoon, Pamela. If there's an urgent call please take a message and ring my cell, especially if it's Ferguson Lynch who should call."

"Absolutely," her assistant chimed.

The phone rang as if on cue and Jama glanced at the digital display and then at her watch. It was Kyle. She'd be late if she picked up, but it had been days since they'd talked. "I'll get this and make it quick. Would you grab the elevator for me?"

"Sure." Pamela hurried from the office.

"Hello. This is Jama." She sat down at her desk.

"Hi. Are you busy?"

"I was on my way out the door to a meeting. I can't talk long. How have you been?"

"Good, a little busy."

"We need to get together again, but I'm not sure when I'll be free this week. Maybe we could do something this weekend?" She twirled a strand of hair around her finger. "Duke's been behaving himself lately. He hasn't made a peep at night."

"That's good. This weekend sounds possible. Millie's been after me to get you back out to dinner. What about Sunday?"

"I can't. I always have Sunday dinner at my mom's, unless you want to join me there?" She bit her bottom lip and closed her eyes. Why had she suggested that? If she brought Kyle home to meet her mom, Lillian would no doubt start thinking they were serious.

"Maybe. I'll let you know. Why don't you call me later when you have more time to talk?"

"Okay."

"Have a good meeting." The line went dead and she hung up. Her stomach knotted. Something was wrong.

Leanne Tyler

She hadn't heard from him in a few days and now that he called, he didn't sound like himself.

Her phone buzzed and the receptionist came over the speaker. "Your elevator is waiting, Ms. Wright."

"I'm on my way." She hurried across the office and out the door, apologizing to her secretary as she got on the elevator. She really wished she hadn't taken Kyle's call now. She couldn't leave things as they were so there was only one thing to do. Call him back.

Once she got into her car she dug her cellphone out of her bag and found her Bluetooth, turning it on. She dialed Kyle's number.

"I thought you had a meeting," he said as soon as he answered.

"I do, but we can talk while I drive." She started her car and pulled out of the parking spot

"If you're sure?"

"I am. How's the vet business?"

"I have a new patient which is always good."

"I like hearing that." She checked her mirrors and merged with the flow of traffic onto the interstate. "I've lined up two more supporters for Kit. And I've talked to a few radio stations about purchasing air-time for commercials. I should have a proposal to you by Friday."

"Speaking of Friday, what does your calendar look like for that evening?" His voice sounded a little uneasy as it had earlier.

"I think I'm free. I'll have to double check. Why?"

"I've got two tickets for a chorus production and wondered if you'd like to go with me? And have dinner with a friend afterward?"

"That's a tentative yes. Call my assistant Pamela when we hang up and have her check my calendar. If I'm free, put it down. Otherwise I might get caught up with work and totally forget by Friday. This week has been a little hectic for me."

"I'll do that."

"Okay. I need to go now. Traffic is a little crazy up ahead and I may need to take an alternate route. Don't eat Hunan with anyone but me."

He laughed. "Be careful."

"Bye."

She ended the call more confident that nothing was wrong. Now she could totally focus on her business meeting.

Kyle hung up the phone and smiled. Everything was good. Jama was going with him Friday night to see Carol's performance and to have dinner with them. He wanted to show Carol that he'd moved on and had found someone to share his life. Maybe he should have explained that to Jama so she'd have known how important Friday night was for him, but he really didn't think a hurried phone call was the time. He'd do it on the way to the performance.

Whistling, he grabbed his bag and went back to the waiting area where Vikki had finished tidying up. She sat behind the counter reading. "You can go early if you want."

Her head popped up from the magazine. "Are you sure? Don't you have that house call to make? Shouldn't I stay here in case we get a walk-in?"

He shrugged. "Or you can stay. If I'm not back by four thirty you can leave, just lock up."

"Gotcha." She saluted him. "You talk to Jama?"

He nodded.

"See. She was happy to hear from you, right?"

"Yeah and I don't think she got my message because she didn't mention it. So you were right about that too. I should have called her again instead of waiting."

Vikki smiled.

"I'll be at the Henderson's if you need me. I have my cell."

Chapter Fourteen

Jama filled Duke's water bowl with fresh water and scooped his daily allotment of food into the other one. He crawled on his haunches over to the bowl too lazy to get up on all fours. She laughed watching him sniff the food to see if he wanted to eat it.

"Have a good day, boy." She opened the gate and went to her car.

Thankfully the drive to work was uneventful. She was the first one in and that was always good. She liked working when it was quiet. After making a pot of coffee, she went to her desk to start on the day's to-do list.

She was on her second cup of coffee when Pamela knocked on her door. "Good morning."

Jama glanced up from reviewing a copy proof. "So far it is."

"That's good. After you left, Kyle Landers called and asked me to schedule him in on your calendar for Friday night."

"Yes. I told him to so I wouldn't forget. There wasn't a conflict, was there?"

"Not then, but I was going through your mail this morning and found this invitation. The postmark indicates you should have received it weeks ago. What should I do?" Pamela handed her the invitation. "Wright & Associates normally purchases a table for this one. I'm surprised they didn't call when we didn't respond."

Jama glanced at the card to the charity event. "We can miss this year. Send them our regrets and have Judith cut them a check for a donation. Any word from Ferguson Lynch?"

"Not yet."

She frowned as Pamela left. It bothered her that Lynch hadn't called. He'd made a point of cornering Judith to arrange a meeting and now that she was receptive to it, there hadn't been a peep.

She pressed her lips together and shook her head. Some men liked to play games in business and she didn't like it. Kyle wasn't a game player. In fact, he was the type of man she'd been hoping to meet for a long time now. She hadn't realized it because she was still getting over Ted dropping his bombshell and turning her life upside down.

Picking up the phone, she dialed Kyle's cell number. She got his voicemail. "Hey it's Jama. Thinking about you and looking forward to Friday night. Call me later and tell me more about this show we're going to see. I can't wait."

Smiling she hung up the phone and went to drop off the proof. As she walked by her assistant's desk, Pamela waved her arms frantically to get her attention. "I just put Lynch on hold. Line two."

"Great! Take this to copy for me."

Her assistant gave her a thumbs-up as she headed back to her office.

She picked up the phone. "This is Jama, can I help you?"

"Ferguson Lynch here."

"Hello, Mr. Lynch. So good to hear from you. My accounting manager tells me you are interested in a meeting. I'm open to a discussion."

"I'm glad to hear that. I think what I have lined up is an excellent fit for your agency."

"I'll be the judge of that. When can I put you on my calendar?"

"Friday at four. I'm having cocktails at Cherokee. Meet me there. If you aren't a member tell them you're my guest"

She rolled her eyes and jotted down the information. "I'll see you then."

It was just like Lynch to plan a meeting at the country club to show off, and that little jab about her not being a member was not winning him any brownie points. She buzzed Pamela and had her add the appointment to her calendar. "What time did Kyle give you for our date?"

"He said six and he'd meet you at the Civic Auditorium if necessary. There's a pre-show reception since it's opening night."

"Okay. Thanks." Surely her meeting with Lynch couldn't last more than an hour at tops. She'd have plenty of time to swing by her condo and change into something more formal for the date. But that would mean no going to Keely's house and taking Duke for his jog. Maybe Kyle would do it for her? She made herself a note to mention it when they talked.

"You're a lifesaver, Kyle." She told him on the phone later that night, stacking the mass of papers that littered the bed where she'd been working. "So tell me more about this production we're going to see."

There was a little silence and she could hear him breathing. "It's a Vegas show. Someone I once knew is in it and she invited me to come see her."

"Oh. I see. Is that why you've sounded a little strange whenever you mentioned it?"

"I guess." More silence. "Look. I'm not exactly eager to go, but if it will add a more solid closure on that chapter in my life, then I'll do it. I want Carol to see her leaving hasn't kept me from having a good life."

Jama put the papers in her brief case and swallowed. "Were you going to tell me about this?"

"Yes."

"When?"

"Friday so you wouldn't back out."

She smiled, finding his confession sweet. She could tell this was difficult for him. "I wouldn't back out. So tell me about Carol."

"Okay." He took a deep breath.

She listened as he explained about his past relationship with this woman who'd left him to go to Vegas to be a show girl. "She has a lot of nerve contacting you now."

"That's what Vikki says."

"For once I agree one hundred percent with your cousin. But don't worry. I'll be there. We'll face seeing Carol again together."

"I'm glad. It's taken me a long time to get to this place in my life and I'm glad I met you."

"Not as glad as I am to have met you." Jama smiled and looked at the clock. "I hate to go, but it's getting late and I have another big day tomorrow. I'll meet you as close to six on Friday as I can. I'll call if I'm running late."

"Okay."

"Goodnight, Kyle. Pleasant dreams."

"Goodnight, Jama."

She hung up the phone and turned out the light before sliding under the thin cover. Closing her eyes, she thought about Kyle and wondered about the type of person Carol was to have treated him that way. She wasn't looking forward to meeting the woman, but she'd do it for his sake.

Pushing the unpleasant thoughts aside, she once again allowed her mind to drift to the vacation she wanted to take. The clear, crystal water and a sandy beach where she could lounge in the sun all day, and do nothing but spend the day with Kyle. Maybe it was time to ask him if he wanted to go on this trip with her. She sure kept fantasizing about him being there.

Friday afternoon Jama walked into the country club prepared with figures and projections Judith had compiled in case Lynch asked. The maître d' showed her to a private dining room off from the main area where the man waited for her. But he wasn't alone. Two other men in sharp tailored suits were having drinks with him around the large circular table that took up most of the room. They stood when she walked in.

"Jama, come join us." Lynch beckoned. "What can I get you to drink?"

"Club soda with lime."

He snapped his fingers and a waiter she hadn't spotted hurried from the room. "I'd like you to meet Mr. Walter Boyd and Mr. Byron Higgins from Crabtree, Boyd & Lane."

She shook their hands noting that Mr. Boyd was the shorter of the two with salt and pepper hair, while Mr.

Higgins with thin and lean, but balding around the crown. Lynch pulled out a chair for her. "It's a pleasure, gentleman. I'm afraid I'm not familiar with your firm."

"That's because we're from New York," Mr. Boyd said.

"Oh?" She glanced at Lynch.

He took his seat again. "Don't be angry with me, Jama, but I thought we'd save a step by having the gentlemen meet with us right away."

She fixed a glare on him, but tried to smile. "You really shouldn't have gone to that trouble. Really. You shouldn't have."

"It's our fault. We were visiting the area and wanted to meet with you." Mr. Higgins set his drink on the table. "We understand your brother is Darren Wright. He worked for our parent company for several years. We were sad to see him go. He had great potential."

"Lynch has been telling us how he helped you turn your agency around after a patch of bad luck," Boyd added. "We'd love to have him work for us again at a regional level. That's why we urged for this meeting."

The waiter brought Jama her drink, and she drained half of it in one gulp. She sat the glass in front of her. "I'm afraid I don't understand. I was under the impression that this meeting was about a possible merger if I was interested in selling. Instead, it sounds like you're interested in stealing Darren away. He's been an asset to Wright & Associates this last year. I'd hate to see him go, but shouldn't you be meeting with him instead of me?"

"We have no intention of stealing him away," Mr. Higgins assured. "We're interested in Wright & Associates as a whole."

"Perhaps we should order another round of drinks and discuss a few options," Lynch suggested.

"Frankly gentlemen, Wright & Associates is not for sale. I took this meeting to hear my options in the event I might be persuaded otherwise. Let's keep this in mind."

Lynch pulled at his shirt collar, gave a nervous chuckle and glared at her this time. "Jama, whatever do you mean?"

"Exactly what I said. I do not intend to sell."

"We understand," Mr. Boyd said. "And we appreciate your telling us upfront. We're prepared to make you a generous offer in the event you do wish to sell and join the Crabtree, Boyd, & Lane family."

She listened to their spiel and looked over the documents they presented. Darren had been right that she'd be allowed to keep the name Wright & Associates, and the day to day running of the agency would be hers, but she'd have to report to New York on a regular basis. During the transition period there would even be an executive from New York joining her agency. She wasn't certain she liked the idea of a big brother agency watching her every move even if the extra backing would give her more freedom to go after higher risk clients.

"Thank you gentlemen." She stood and shook their hands again. "You've given me much to consider."

Kyle glanced at his watch again. It was going on eight o'clock. Jama had promised she'd call if she were going to be late. She hadn't and he was beginning to worry. She wasn't picking up her cellphone either.

The lights in the lobby of the Civic Auditorium dimmed letting the patrons know the show was about to start. He lingered until the lobby was empty and then he called her cellphone one last time. It went straight to voicemail.

"Jama. It's Kyle. Where are you? I'm worried. Give me a call as soon as you get this."

He flipped his phone closed, and turned to go find his seat.

"Kyle!" He heard her voice and turned back to see her rushing toward him in a bright pink strapless, sequined dress that came to just above the knees. Her hair was piled up on her head, and sparkling earrings dangled from her earlobes. Seeing her dressed like that made him want to forget the show and meeting up with Carol.

"I'm so sorry. My afternoon meeting turned into an ambush and I lost track of the time."

"You said you'd call. I was worried."

"I know, but my cell battery died. I forgot my charger at home. I swear I don't know where my head is these days. I really do need to take a vacation."

He pulled her into his arms and smelled the sweet raspberry scent she wore. "The important thing is you are here and you're okay. Let's go find out seats. Unless you'd rather I sent my regrets backstage and we go somewhere we can be alone."

She giggled. "Mr. Landers are you suggesting—"

He shrugged.

She leaned into him and kissed him, running her hand up his neck sending tingles down his spine. "I'd like nothing better, but I don't want you not showing to send the wrong message to Carol."

With a sigh, he said, "Okay. Let's go find our seats then."

She slipped her arm through his and they walked to the doorway, giving the usher their tickets. The houselights dimmed as they were shown to their seats. The orchestra began playing and the curtains slowly rose on an array of colorful dancing girls. Jama crossed her legs and her dress rose higher, showing off her thigh.

He leaned toward her ear. "I like your dress."

She smiled. "Thanks. I rarely get to wear it, but I thought tonight would be perfect since it's opening night."

"You look great in it, did I mention that?"

She shook her head and took his hand, entwining her fingers with his. "I'm glad you like it."

"I think I would like you even more without it on."

"Kyle!" She swiveled in her seat to look at him. "What has gotten into you?"

"I'm just being honest."

She leaned closer and whispered. "Maybe you'd like me better in a bikini on the beach?"

"Maybe."

"Think about it."

She turned back to watch the show, but his mind was not on the scantily clad women dancing on stage, but on what she'd suggested. Jama in a bikini. He blew out his breath and shook his head.

Somehow he made it through the show and they headed to the side entrance to meet up with Carol. She still wore her headdress and costume of sequins and rhinestones. Her six-inch beaded heels made her taller than him.

"Oh Kyle. It's so good to see you. I was afraid you'd not come, even though you accepted the tickets I sent."

"How are you?" he asked, squeezing Jama's hand tighter.

"I'm wonderful. Couldn't be better. You know how I always wanted to be a dancer. Now here I am." She smiled and looked from him to Jama. She extended her hand. "Hello. I'm Carol Haney and you must be?"

"Jama Wright." She pulled her hand away from Kyle's grasp to shake hands with Carol. "I enjoyed the show. Thanks for inviting us."

"My pleasure. Are we still on for dinner?" she asked, reaching up to remove the beaded and plumed headdress she wore.

"Y-yes. Anywhere you want to go." Kyle wrapped his arm around Jama's waist.

"Give me about five minutes and I'll meet you back here."

When she was gone Jama cupped his face in her hands. "You did fine. Don't be nervous."

"Sorry if I came on a little strong in there with the reference to your dress." His face warmed now that he thought of her reaction to what he'd said.

"Don't be sorry. It's nice to know you are that attracted to me. I was just surprised. You've never said anything like that before and in all honesty I'm wondering if it wasn't prompted by us being here to see Carol."

He groaned. "Maybe coming here tonight wasn't a good idea after all."

"No. I think it was a right move. And I'm glad you asked me to be here for you. I know if Ted Donaldson ever came back wanting to meet me, I'd like you to be here for me."

"He's the one who stole money from your agency, right?"

"Yes." She smiled. "But we were involved too. I don't think I told you that."

He nodded. "No. You didn't. So he not only robbed you but he broke your heart when he left."

"Yes, but looking back now that the anger and hurt is gone, I think it was a relief when he left. We were comfortable together. No spark. No emotion. I've never been in a relationship where I feel like I'm with my other half until now."

He smiled. Was she saying what he thought she was? "Am I your other half?"

She wrapped her arms around his neck. "I believe you are, Mr. Landers."

He pulled her closer and kissed her. "I'm glad to know you feel this way because I do too."

"I'm ready," Carol sang and they stepped apart. "My, Kyle, but you two look fabulous together and you're obviously happy. I'm glad because I didn't leave you on good terms. I'm sorry. I hope you can forgive me.

"That's really what I wanted to tell you. I'm so glad you agreed to meet me so I could. I want to move on with my life and it was important for me to say that. You see I've met someone myself. And we're getting married. Tony couldn't make this trip with me. He's a plastic surgeon."

Kyle swallowed. A plastic surgeon. Why didn't that surprise him? It explained her ugly, fuller lips. "I forgave you a long time ago, but I appreciate your apology and I wish you and Tony all the happiness."

"Thanks. I know you said we'd go to eat anywhere I wanted. I hope you don't mind, but I made reservations for us at a steak house around the corner. I'm normally ravenous after a show and I wanted to go somewhere close. Have you ever been to the Ruth Chris' in town before?"

"Yes. Nice choice. You won't be disappointed," Jama told her.

"Oh good. I'm glad to hear it. National chain restaurants can be so different from city to city. It's close enough to walk. Let's go."

Chapter Fifteen

Jama put Duke in his yard after an early morning jog. She had lots to do for a Saturday and didn't want to cause him to miss out on his daily exercise. Opening the door to the kitchen the ringing of the telephone greeted her. She dropped her keys on the counter and grabbed the receiver. "Wright-Jones residence."

"Jama," Darren said. "How's it going? I haven't heard from you. Did you meet with Lynch?"

She cradled the receiver between her shoulder and her ear, opened up the refrigerator door and grabbed a bottle of water. "Yes. Yesterday evening. Sorry I didn't get to call you last night. I had a date afterward and we got in late. I figured you and Keely wouldn't appreciate my calling you if you were, ahem, otherwise engaged."

"Funny. So tell me what did Lynch say?"

She sighed. "First he said let's have cocktails at the country club. So I go expecting to have a brief chat with the man, but that isn't what happened. He invited me there to meet up with the New York agency that is interested in merging."

"That's underhanded. Did you walk out?"

"No. I think I handled myself well. I made it clear I wasn't interested in selling. I was only there to hear what they had to say. But that isn't even the best part. Do you know who the agency that is interested in the merger is?"

"How would I?"

"Guess."

"I don't have a clue."

"Darren, think about it."

"Just tell me before my cell battery dies."

"Crabtree, Boyd, and Lane. And they are very interested in you."

Silence filled the airwaves for a few seconds before she heard him groan. "What do they want?"

"I first thought they were looking to steal you away, but they want more of the pie. They want the whole agency as well. I have a proposal and a dossier explaining the merger package. If you insist on seeing it I will have Pamela send an electronic version to you on Monday."

"You aren't considering it, are you?"

"No. At this time I'm not. Unless you think I should."

"Remember I told you a few mergers went badly?"

"Yes."

"That was putting it mildly. Do not walk, run in the other direction. Who did they send to meet with you?"

"Boyd and Higgins."

She heard swearing on the other end.

"Lynch will regret the day he set that meeting up."

"Should I go into the office and send you the documents today?"

"No need. I doubt they've changed the boilerplate. Now I wish I hadn't encouraged you to meet with Lynch."

"Hey, it was a meeting. Nothing more. A few hours wasted, but at least I know what I'm up against if they press the issue."

"Yeah. And they will. Jackson and Jackson called me a head hunter when I was first seeing Keely. I wasn't, but those two men are, they've hunted you down and got you in their sights. Be careful until I get back. If you resist their courting they may try to play hardball. If they do, you call me immediately. I know their game plan."

Jama swallowed. She didn't like what he was insinuating. "I will. Thanks for the heads up."

"No problem. Gotta run. We've got a water tour of the island today. I think you should consider coming here on your vacation. It's really been nice. They have time-shares here too. Maybe we should consider it. It could be a company perk for the executives."

"A time-share? Darren, do you think that would be wise?"

"It's something to think about."

"I haven't decided yet where I'll go on vacation, but I'll keep it in mind. Tell Keely hello for me."

"I will. See you in about a week."

"Okay." She hung up the phone and finished her bottle of water as she went upstairs to take a quick shower. She had about an hour or more of work to do before meeting Kyle for the afternoon. He'd persuaded her to go out to the McDougal's with him again today and he had promised to go to Sunday dinner at her mom's tomorrow.

She really didn't mind going to the McDougal farm. She liked the couple very much, even if Millie came on a little strong. However, she wasn't as easy minded about him meeting her mom. Lillian would jump to the conclusion that they were a serious couple even if Jama explained to her mom otherwise. But it didn't matter if she did it now or later, the result would be the same. Therefore she really didn't need to worry it.

Brushing her hair back, she twisted it into a loose bun and clamped it into place with a large clip. After slipping into lounging pants and a tank, she headed downstairs in her bare feet to make a light snack before settling into work. Her cell phone rang and she grabbed it anticipating the caller to be Kyle, but it wasn't.

"Jama, Fred McDaniel here. I hope I haven't caught you at a bad time, but I've heard something very disturbing and I can't wait until Monday to discuss it with you."

"I'm glad you called then." She swallowed and tried to keep her voice from conveying alarm even though her eye twitched from panic. Whatever he'd heard had to be bad because Fred McDaniel had never called her on her cell even though she'd given him her number months ago after Darren signed the account.

"I ran into Ferguson Lynch last evening and he was telling me how Wright & Associates was going to become part of a larger New York firm. He even introduced me to the fellas from New York."

Jama opened her mouth to speak but no sound came out. When her voice returned she spoke gibberish. "H-he what?"

"I didn't like them. I don't want to be owned by New York, and frankly I'm surprised that you'd even consider going this route. I've given this some thought and I'll have to pull my account from Wright & Associates and go with a local firm. I'm sorry it has come to this, but I find this whole ordeal very underhanded."

"You'll what?"

"I'm sure *more* of your clients will feel the same way when they hear."

She swallowed. "Listen Mr. McDaniel…Fred, I haven't signed anything. I only took a meeting with Ferguson Lynch as a courtesy, but I have no intention of allowing a merger of any sort. I can't help what false information he is spreading."

"I wasn't the only client that learned this news last night. Gleason from Kernell was there, and he told me you had just met, but hadn't mentioned anything to him. He was hot under the collar."

"What can I do to reassure you that I'm not merging?" Jama's temple throbbed and she grabbed a notepad from her briefcase. She wrote frantically on it making a list of everyone she could think of that was on her client list, putting a star by those who were also members of the country club. She feared how many Lynch may have poisoned with his news. Only a few names came to mind, but enough to cause major damage.

"I like having my business contacts local," McDaniel rattled. "That's why when I moved to Knoxville and moved with my distribution center here, I shopped for an agency to handle my business."

"And you've been happy with our services for the last year. Darren has met every request you've had head on. I can assure you Wright & Associates is committed to you and will continue to provide the same if not better service in the future."

"I'd like to believe that, but those fellas from New York boasted about how your brother once worked for their parent company. How do I know he didn't come here as a way to bridge your agency with Crabtree, Boyd, and Lane?"

She winced. "I know that sounds bad, but Darren hasn't even spoken to his former agency. He's on his honeymoon. You were at the wedding."

"I know I was, but he did steal his bride away from Jackson and Jackson."

"Keely left Jackson and Jackson on good terms when she fell in love with my brother. He didn't steal her away. She didn't want to work for an opposing firm where they'd be competitors."

"Someone should tell Jackson and Jackson that because they found what Lynch was spouting last night very interesting too. They're the ones that made the connection between these New York fellas and Darren. I didn't like feeling I'd been caught with my pants down around my ankles."

Wow. A visual she did not need. Eew. She silently groaned and added the Jacksons to her list of names. The competition between her firm and theirs had subsided a little after Keely joined the agency. But she sensed that truce had ended after what Lynch told everyone within hearing distance last night. They'd no doubt be trying to sign any of her clients that wanted to part ways.

"Can we meet in person and talk this afternoon? I'd feel better if we did," she said laying down her pen.

"I don't want to ruin your day. I'm sure you have more important things to do on a Saturday than attend to business."

She immediately thought of Kyle and their plans to go to the McDougals. Surely he'd understand she couldn't let this situation escalate. She needed to squelch the troubled waters before they became a tidal wave wiping out her life's work.

"It is Saturday, but taking care of your concerns is more important than anything else I might have planned for the day."

"I do appreciate your willingness to see me."

"Will two o'clock work for you? Just name the place and I'll be there."

"I'm playing golf with Gleason at the country club. Why don't you come along and we can talk. You do play, don't you?"

"A little."

"I'll see you there."

The call ended and she hurried upstairs to change into street clothes so she could go to her condo and find her golf shoes. She dialed Kyle's cell, but he didn't answer. She didn't leave a voice mail preferring to talk to him when she cancelled their plans.

Kyle pulled a clean shirt over his head coming out of the bathroom. His cell rang and he went to the chest where he'd left it. It was Jama.

"Hey beautiful. Can't wait to see me?"

"Listen Kyle something major has come up with work. I'm going to have to cancel today."

She sounded stressed and he knew that couldn't be good. "It's Saturday. Your day off. Can't this wait until Monday?"

"Normally I'd agree, but my world is crashing down around me. I don't have time to explain, just know I'm sorry. Send my regrets to the McDougals."

"Is there anything I can do to help?"

"No. I made this mess and only I can clear it up. Thanks for understanding."

"What about tomorrow? Are we still going to your mom's?"

"I…I'll have to get back to you on that. I might have to cancel with my mom too."

"Okay. Call me later."

"I will if I can. Bye."

The line went dead and he snapped his cell shut. He didn't like what he was hearing. She was shutting him out. Her business was more important than him, her friends, and her family. When would Jama learn that she didn't have to do this alone?

He grabbed his keys and headed to the door. Just because Jama couldn't go with him today didn't mean he had to cancel on the McDougals as well. He got in his Jeep and drove, thinking about how he'd planned to take her horseback riding. He'd also wanted to show her those kittens in the barn loft and how relaxing lying on a bed of hay could feel while you did nothing but stare up at the cobwebs. But that wasn't going to happen now.

He hit the steering wheel hard with the palm of his hand and wondered what had transpired to make Jama feel like her world was crashing around her. She'd shown up late for their date last night, hadn't kept her word about calling. He believed her when she said her cell phone battery died. It had happened to him enough times with his charger handy. But what kind of urgent business could come up on a weekend to take her away from their plans? And why wouldn't she let him help her? Sure he wasn't in advertising, but there had to be something he could do to help.

Turning off the main road, he barreled up the dirt drive sending billowy dust in his wake. He shouldn't let Jama's not coming today cause his mood to be so sour, but he couldn't help it. This was really bugging him. Slowing down, he pulled to a stop and shut off the motor. He hit the steering wheel with his hand again and leaned his head against it wondering if maybe he should have stayed home.

"What's wrong?" Hank asked.

Kyle's looked up at him.

"I thought you were bringing Jama with you." Hank motioned past him to the empty passenger seat.

"I was, but she couldn't make it at the last minute."

"I see. Too bad. Come into the barn with me. I'm replacing a shoe on one of my horses. I noticed it this morning when I cleaned out her stall. She was fine yesterday when Millie and I went for a sunset ride. There's nothing prettier than watching the sun set over the ridge. You should bring Jama out sometime and take her up there."

Kyle grunted. Fat chance she'd actually show up if he did. "Maybe."

"No maybe about it. You need to." Hank handed him a hammer and a few nails from the tackle room on the right as they entered the barn. "You want to do the honors?"

He shrugged.

"You better get over your mood before we head to the house or Millie will be all over you wanting details."

He placed the hammer under his arm and ran his hand through his hair. "Sorry. Don't know why I'm letting this get to me."

"I do." Hank patted the horse on the rump before he backed up to the mare and pulled her leg up between his legs to hold it still while he worked.

"Why?"

The man grinned. "You like her and wanted to be here with her today. Now you're here alone and that bites. Am I right?"

Kyle nodded and handed him the hammer.

"Your ego is bruised a little too, I'd say."

Yeah. It hurt that Jama shut him out. That she didn't want him to help her.

"Millie stood me up a few times when we were dating. She had younger siblings to care for since her mom died and sometimes her pa couldn't get home from work early enough for us to go out." Hank removed the damaged shoe and took a file from his overalls pocket. He scrapped and smoothed the hoof so the shoe would lay flush. "It caused problems until I realized she was doing what was right. She was providing for her family and if I really cared about her I'd have to be patient, otherwise it wasn't going to work out between us. She couldn't change her role in the family, no more than Jama can change the fact that she is the owner of her business."

He put the file back in his pocket and took the new shoe from the bib pocket. Lining it up on the hoof, he reached his hand out. "Nail."

Kyle gave him the nail and waited for him to hammer it in a few times before giving him the next one.

"No matter why Jama couldn't come today, I'm sure it was important for her to cancel or she'd be here with you now."

"Yeah."

Hank let the horse's leg fall back in place. He patted the mare on the rump again and led her back to her stall. "Let's head up to the house before Millie comes looking for us."

Kyle followed him out of the barn and saw Millie waving from the front porch, one hand on her hip. As they got closer he could see a frown on her face, and he braced himself for her questioning.

"I thought Jama was coming," she said, hugging him as soon as he stepped onto the porch.

"She was but something came up at work that she had to take care of."

"Well pooh. I made a fresh batch of my freezer strawberry jam this week, and I wanted to give her some. Do you think she likes freezer jam?"

"I don't know." He thought about that and realized there were lots he didn't know about Jama that he probably should learn. "But you know I do."

"Don't worry. I made you a care package to take home too. Come on in the house and get washed up. The biscuits should be about ready to come out of the oven."

"I'm going to go wash up and change before we eat." Hank headed toward the stairs.

"Please do. You smell like that barn." Millie winked at Kyle and motioned for him to follow her to the kitchen. "So what did Jama say came up?"

"She didn't. Only that her world was crashing around her, and it couldn't wait until Monday. Nor did she need my help."

"That doesn't sound good."

He washed his hands before he sat on the stool at the counter.

Millie opened the oven and took out the biscuits, transferring them from the pan to the bread basket. "I'm sure Jama is wishing she was here with you instead of doing what is keeping her away. Even though I only met her once, I could tell she is very responsible person, organized. If something urgent came up with her business then she felt she had to take care of it instead of spend the day with us. I respect her for it."

Kyle snatched a biscuit from the basket and Millie smacked at his hand, but he pulled away before she touched him. He hadn't really expected her to take Jama's side on this. Maybe he had been looking at it wrong.

"I think I'll make her a plate of food that you can take to her tonight. I'm sure if she's busy she won't have time to cook for herself."

"She can't cook."

Millie stared at him a moment. "She can't?"

He shook his head.

"Well…that's a pickle."

He smiled, breaking a chunk of biscuit off to pop into his mouth. "That's how I ended up in the ER."

"Because of the takeout. I didn't realize it was because she couldn't cook that you were eating it." Millie shook her head. "Don't you worry. I'll teach her how if she's up to learning."

Hank appeared in the kitchen doorway, hair wet and combed back, wearing clean clothes and smelling of aftershave. "I'm starved. Let's eat."

Millie handed him the bread basket. "Take that out to the dining room and I'll get the tea. Everything else is already on the table getting cold."

"I hurried."

"I know you did."

Kyle followed them to the dining room and took his usual spot, noticing the extra place set for Jama across from him. He filled his plate with the food passed to him and hoped she was having success salvaging things.

Jama dropped her purse on the counter and sat down in the nearest chair to remove her shoes. Her back hurt and her neck was stiff. It had been a long time since she'd played golf, and having to try to convince two angry businessmen that their faith in her agency was a sound investment didn't help matters. Her stomach rumbled, and she headed to the refrigerator to see what frozen entrée she could heat up in the microwave fast for dinner.

A knock at her back door caused her to detour from her destination. Through the open blinds, she thought it looked like Kyle. She opened the door and smiled. "Hi."

"Are you hungry?" He held a plate covered in aluminum.

"How'd you know? I was just about to pop something frozen into the microwave. That smells yummy."

"I guess I have good timing, sometimes."

She heard the sarcasm in his voice, but dismissed it. "Come on in. Have you eaten? Is there enough there for two?"

"I've eaten, thanks. Millie felt bad that you couldn't join us and wanted to make sure you didn't have to worry about cooking on top of everything else. Is that a golf outfit you're wearing?"

"Yeah. I had to meet a couple of clients on the golf course. They could ruin my day, but couldn't give up their golf game."

He handed her the plate. "You'll want to heat it up. We ate a few hours ago, but Millie kept the plate warm in the oven until I left. But I was in the Jeep with the top down so I think it defeated her efforts."

"No problem." She removed the cover and took the plate to the microwave. "Have a seat at the table. We can talk while I eat. I made raspberry tea this morning. Do you want a glass?"

"No. I really should be going. I'm sure you have plenty of work to still resolve."

Jama's brow furrowed. "Are you mad at me?"

"I'm trying not to be, but I find the fact that you've been playing golf instead of spending the day with me a little hard to swallow. What was so earth shattering about that?"

"I wasn't playing golf for fun. I was trying to persuade two of my clients that the garbage they heard last night wasn't true. The man I met with told them I had agreed to sell my business to a New York agency. I didn't do anything other than meet with him to hear about their offer. In hindsight I should never have taken the meeting. I didn't want to sell my agency, but I thought, if it would give me more freedom to spend time with you, then it was worth my time to look into it."

"You'd do that?"

"I was looking at my options."

The microwave dinged and she opened the door, removing the plate. She set in on the counter and turned back to him. "Believe me when I say I would have much rather been with you than doing what I did today."

"You were late for our date last night. You didn't call like you promised. You cancelled today. I see a pattern forming that your business comes before everything else in your life, and it worries me that you'd put it before your family, if we had one."

She crossed her arms and leaned back against the counter, thinking over his words. He was talking like they were getting married. They'd just started dating. Sure she'd been thinking along the lines of something more with him, but marriage?

She took a deep breath and tried to not panic, pushing those thoughts aside. "I have to make sacrifices for my business and the greatest is my time. Wright & Associates is everything to me and I have to give more of myself there, but I'm trying to make it possible to give less. It just isn't easy, especially with Darren away. He's my creative director, but he's also my brother, and I can trust him to do what's best for the agency. He can take over if I needed him. I can give him more responsibility when he returns, freeing me up for more personal time."

"But won't that cause problems for him and Keely?"

"Maybe, but she'd understand being an executive as well."

"So you're saying I don't understand what you're going through because I'm not in advertising? I own my own business. I get house calls late at night. It just hasn't happened when we're together or caused me to cancel on you, yet."

"No. That's not what I'm saying."

"It sure sounds like it." He crossed his arms over his chest. "You didn't want my help earlier when I offered."

"There wasn't anything you could do. I had to go talk to the men."

"And play golf."

Why was he being so unreasonable about this? She turned to the cabinet and took a glass down, went to the refrigerator and got some ice from the freezer and filled her glass with tea. "I wasn't playing golf to be playing. It was strictly business."

"I could have played golf."

"You play?"

"No, but how hard could it be to hit that little ball."

"Harder than it looks. I took lessons in college because one of my business professors said it would pay off to know how one day. And it has several times."

He sat down at the table, but didn't say anything.

Jama collected her plate, grabbed a fork from the drawer and came to the table to sit. "Look. I understand you are frustrated by the way things have gone today. I am too. But it won't always be like this."

"How can you guarantee?"

"I can't and I won't. I grew up having no one to rely on but me. I learned there are no guarantees when your father walks out on his family and leaves a wife with four kids alone. Patty and Claire, my twin sisters, cooked and cleaned and I took care of them and Darren, while our mom worked two jobs. Not a picture of bliss, but we survived. Thankfully mom is retired now and doing well on her own. Patty and Claire run a lodge in the Blue Ridge Mountains, and Darren and I work in advertising."

She took a drink of her tea. "So maybe you can see why I'm a workaholic now. I've always had to work. To put my needs second for the sake of others. It isn't easy to change, even if I do try to take baby steps."

Kyle nodded, feeling like a heel. He got up from the table and kissed her on the head. "I'm sorry for not understanding."

She grabbed his hand. "It's okay. We've both been through some emotional stress these last few days. Carol coming to town and my work keeping me busy."

"Yeah. I guess you're right."

She stood and wrapped her arms around his neck. "Sometimes it is hard to be weak and let someone else be strong for me. If I ever make you feel like I'm pushing you away, please tell me."

He leaned his forehead to rest against hers, his gut clenching tight with remorse for the way he'd been feeling all day. "You did today, but I understand now."

"I'm sorry."

He brushed his lips against hers and she tilted her head up to deepen the kiss when the sound of Duke's howling bark interrupted them.

"Not now," Jama groaned.

"I'll go check on him, you eat."

"Thanks."

He hurried outside and found the dog underneath the tree, howling at nothing as far as he could see. He took a scoop of kibble from the bin and went into the back yard to feed him. Headlights flashed as a white Cadillac SUV pulled up beside his Jeep. A woman he didn't recognize got out and waved to him.

"Hello, Kyle."

Her Cajun accent was thick and she wore a flowing colorful skirt and peasant top with several bangle bracelets on her arms.

"Hi."

"Is Jama in the house?"

"Yeah. In the kitchen."

"Be a dear and get my suitcase for me. It's in the back."

"Is she expecting you?"

"Probably not. How's Duke?"

"Right now? Fine."

"Good." She went to the back porch, knocked on the door and went inside.

Duke flopped down, resting his jaws on Kyle's foot. He looked down at the dog and scratched his head, wondering who that woman was.

Chapter Sixteen

"Lucinda!" Jama exclaimed, putting down her fork. "I wondered when I'd see you again."

"I know. I know. My two-week stint in New England turned into three. I had the opportunity to do a few extra shows and thought why not. How have you been? I see the vet is here visiting with Duke. Have things been going good with him?"

"The dog or Kyle?"

Lucinda laughed and clapped her hands. "Kyle silly."

"Up until today great, but ..."

"Yes. I had a feeling as I was driving here that today has been trying for you both. That looks like a delicious dish you're eating. Did you make it?"

"No. Millie McDougal did. Kyle brought it to me. We were supposed to go there today, but I had something come up for work. Do you want some tea?" Jama stood and headed to the cabinet.

"I'd love a glass." Lucinda sat at the end of the table and fanned herself with her hand and her bangle bracelets jingled. "So did you get my present?"

"Yes. I loved it. Where did you ever find it?"

"A little shop in New England. It reminded me of one a fan sent me. I thought you'd like it."

"It plays a wonderful tune. Did you know it did that?"

"Some enchanted evening. When you find your true love…" Lucinda recited the lyrics moving her arms in time with the tune, her bracelets jingling. "Ah, and did you find your true love that most romantic evening?"

Jama swirled around. "What do you know about that night?"

Lucinda laughed. "Everything."

"Then you know all there is to know." Jama reached up and touched the gris-gris. "This thing glows and heats, and chills. Did you know that?"

"Yes. And what has it taught you?"

"That even I am susceptible to falling in love. That even a workaholic like me can be sidetracked by wanting what the heart wants. But I don't know that I'm ready for more than spending time with him. He said some things tonight that scared me."

"No one said you had to make a life-time commitment right away. That isn't what the gris-gris does, Jama. It only brings you and your soul mate together. Helps you see the truth before you."

The woman smiled and Jama took the glass from the cabinet and went to the refrigerator to get her tea.

"You haven't fought the gris-gris the way Keely did. She was a stubborn thing fighting its powers. But not you. You've allowed it to guide you, accepting what is meant to be and there is nothing you should be scared about. Kyle is the one for you. He isn't ready to commit yet either, but he is wanting to, just like you. Be patient. Love is, you know."

Jama closed the refrigerator door and brought the tea over to the table. She sat down again. "I guess the real test is how he'll hold up meeting my mom for the first time tomorrow."

Lucinda laughed again. "That should be interesting. I'm glad I'll be there."

"You will?"

She nodded. "Yes. You're mom invited me to join you. We talk regularly now. Have been ever since we met at the lodge when I tricked Keely into going away for that fateful weekend."

Jama recalled her role in making that weekend at Patty and Claire's lodge happen. She'd sent Darren and her mom there and then enlisted Lucinda to make sure Keely was there as well. That was where Darren and Keely's relationship finally came together.

The backdoor opened and Kyle came inside pulling a large rollaway. "Where do you want it?"

"The guest room at the top of the stairs. And will you bring in the trunk as well. I might need it too." Lucinda smiled.

"You got it." He headed to the living room and the stairs.

"You're staying here?" Jama asked when he was out of hearing distance.

"I always stay here when I'm in town. Didn't Keely tell you?"

"No. But okay. I can always use help with Duke."

Lucinda patted her hand. "Don't worry. I won't be in your way. I have things to do, people to see. But I don't do dogs."

"Neither did *I* before I came here."

Lucinda laughed, then smiled. "He's a very handsome young man. I knew the first time I spoke to him on the phone he was just right for you."

"But we hadn't met yet. How could you know?"

The woman shrugged and reached for her tea. She took a drink and set the glass down. "Some things are better left a mystery, my dear. I think I'll take my tea upstairs and have a shower. I've been traveling a long distance and could use some refreshing. Besides, I'm sure you and Kyle would like a few moments alone."

"Okay." When Lucinda was gone, Jama gathered the dishes and headed to the sink. Spending time with her was going to be different, but maybe she needed a little different around here.

"Who is that woman?" Kyle asked coming back into the kitchen.

"Lucinda. She's a family friend of Keely's. Don't you remember talking to her on the phone? She had you come and watch Duke one weekend so she could take Keely away."

"That was over a year ago, but I do remember now. She told me to ask you if I can put her trunk in the living room."

"Sure."

"Are we okay?" he asked.

"Yes. We are just fine. You still up for dinner at my mom's tomorrow?"

He nodded. "If you're sure business won't get in the way."

"I think I took care of their worries today, and I'm hoping they will share this info with any of my other clients who may have overheard the same BS from Ferguson Lynch."

"I hope you're right. I guess I better go get Lucinda's trunk."

"Thank you."

Jama rinsed her plate and glass and put them in the dishwasher before she headed into the living room to find a place for the trunk. Kyle carried it into the room and she directed him over to the corner. "Set it at an angle so it looks like it belongs there, not just stowed out of the way."

He set it down. "It wasn't too heavy, just large. I wonder what she has in there."

"Potions and incense … that kind of stuff."

He chuckled. "Do you think?"

She shrugged and grabbed his hand, leading him over to the sofa. "Sit with me."

He sat down and she snuggled up beside him, leaning her head against his shoulder. He wrapped his arm around her and pulled her close. "This is nice."

"Yes." She closed her eyes and breathed in the outdoors mingled with a hint of hay and wondered what he'd done today at the McDougals, but didn't dare ask. She didn't want to start another discussion, semi-argument about her not going with him. Instead she thought about her vacation plans and how she really wanted to get away from things.

"Kyle," she raised her head to look up at him. "Do you like the beach?"

"Sure. Why?"

"I'm going to take my first vacation in a long time, and I'm thinking about going to the Caribbean or someplace exotic."

"That sounds nice. I'm sure you'll have a good time."

"I think I'd have an even better time if you went too. Would you want to come?"

He smiled. "Is that why you mentioned me seeing you in a bikini the other night?"

She nodded. "I know I might be rushing things, but every time I think about the vacation, I imagine you there with me. So I thought maybe you might want to go?"

"Let me think about it."

"Okay." She leaned back against his shoulder. "We'd do separate accommodations."

"Naturally."

"I think we'd have fun."

"I think we would too."

"Is that a yes?" She raised her head to look at him again.

"Do you have a date in mind yet?"

She shook her head. "It would have to be after Keely and Darren return, and whenever I can get a reservation."

"I'd have to get someone to cover my clinic since I work alone, but I think I could do it. Vikki will enjoy having some time off."

Jama smiled and leaned toward him. He met her halfway and kissed her. The gris-gris grew warm against her skin as he pulled her closer.

"Do you know if Keely still has chamomile tea in the kitchen?" Lucinda said from the stairs. "Oh…uh…Sorry to interrupt."

They pulled apart and Jama laid her head back on his shoulder, taking a deep breath. "No, I don't."

"Never mind. I'll find it if there is any. Go back to what you were doing." Lucinda hurried out of the room.

"I think I better go." Kyle got up off the sofa. "What time are we supposed to be at your mom's tomorrow?"

"Two. Come over about one thirty and we'll go. Lucinda will be joining us. Mom invited her."

"Good. Less pressure on us."

Jama snickered. "You haven't met my mom yet."

"No, but I got through the evening with Carol. I think I can get through this."

"True." She stood and walked him to the front door. "Drive careful."

He touched her face in a gentle caress and ran his thumb over her lips. "I'll see you tomorrow."

"See you." She closed the door behind him and leaned against it. She could hear Lucinda opening and closing cabinet doors in the kitchen so she went to help her find the tea.

Kyle pulled on a clean shirt and buttoned it up before tucking it into his casual pants. He combed his still damp hair before he headed out the door. There was a tightness in his chest that he assumed was nerves. He'd felt something similar before going to the show to meet up with Carol again. Meeting Jama's mother shouldn't be a big deal, but it was for him. He wanted the woman to like him, and he needed to make a good impression.

The drive to Jama's took a little longer than he expected for a Sunday afternoon, but church services in the area had let out and many families were heading to local restaurants for lunch. That made him wonder what Jama's mom had prepared for them to eat. Had Jama thought to inform her mom that he was allergic to chili peppers? He couldn't afford another trip to the ER so soon.

Turning off of Cedar lane into Jama's drive, he noticed that the white Cadillac SUV wasn't there. Had Lucinda left already? He spotted Jama in the back yard with Duke. She wore a pretty sundress and had her hair pulled up on the back of her head in a twist. He cut the engine, got out, and watched her toss a Frisbee for Duke to go fetch. The dog lumbered along for a few feet and flopped down to chew on the edges of the plastic.

"Bring it here, Duke. Don't eat it," she called, but the dog didn't pay her any attention. She walked over and wrestled it free from his hold. "Fine. If you are going to be that way then we're through playing."

Kyle finally walked through the backyard to where she stood. "Hi."

"Hey." She looked back at him and then swung around to do a double-take of his appearance. "Wow. You clean up nice, Mr. Landers. I've never seen you in anything but jeans before."

He grinned, rubbing his hand up the back of his neck. "Glad you approve."

"You know I do." She threw the Frisbee over to the shade of the oak tree where Duke normally lay and the lazy dog slowly got up and trotted over there. "Let me go wash my hands and lock up and I'll be ready to go."

"Where's Lucinda?"

"Already over at mom's. She is making her delectable beignets for dessert so she had to go to the store to get the ingredients and went on over to start preparing them."

"About lunch today. I got to thinking—"

"Don't worry, I told mom you are allergic to chili peppers and I mentioned it to Lucinda to make sure she didn't decide to make another Cajun dish to go with the meal. Do you know she had the nerve to laugh at me because I can't cook? Not that you ended up in the ER, but because I can't cook and that is why you ended up there."

He grinned. "As long as she was clear no chili peppers, she can laugh all she wants."

"Gee, thanks." Jama winked. "She can make fun of me all she wants and you're okay with it. Is that it?"

"Yeah."

She shook her head. "Will you make sure Duke has enough water until I get back? I won't be a minute."

"Sure." He walked over to the water spigot and turned on the water then picked up the hose and let a little water run out of it before he filled the large bowl for the dog. He turned the spigot back off and headed to the Jeep to put the rag top up so Jama's hair wouldn't get windblown as he drove.

"You didn't have to do that," she called, coming up behind him.

"Yes I did. I like your hair up like that. I don't want it messed up."

"Thank you." She kissed him on the cheek and hurried to the passenger side to climb inside. "I have exciting news. I got online this morning and found us an all-inclusive resort that has a suite with two bedrooms. The best part is they're running a special so I got a great deal on the week long package. I just need to confirm before midnight tonight and it's ours."

"Where is the resort?" he asked.

"Montego Bay."

"Sounds good." He started the engine and slowly backed up to turn before pulling out of the drive.

"Darren had wanted me to go to the same place he and Keely went on their honeymoon to check out a possible time share location, but I'd rather go somewhere different. Besides, I'm going for relaxation. I don't want to be thinking about business."

With the top up, it made it easier for them to talk and he listened as Jama rambled on about the trip. The price of the trip wasn't bad either for a last-minute trip this time of year. He'd just need to clear his schedule for that week, but that shouldn't be too difficult.

Between details about the trip, she gave him directions to her mom's retirement community. Lucinda's SUV was parked in the drive and he pulled in behind her. "What if she doesn't like me?"

Jama laughed. "How could she not? You're adorable."

Adorable? He never thought others saw him that way. He sure didn't think that about himself. Adorable was a word he'd use to describe a pet, or a child.

He got out of the Jeep and came around the help her out.

"Relax, Kyle. Mom will like you. She likes everyone."

Everyone?

Jama took his hand and led him to the front door. She rang the bell and within a few seconds it opened.

"You're here!" the petite woman said, beaming. "I thought you'd never get here. Come in out of the heat. You must be Kyle. I'm Lillian. Jama said you are a veterinarian."

"Yes, ma'am."

"She also said you're a country boy who likes meat and potatoes. So I've fixed a country meal. Come on into the kitchen. Lucinda is taking up the cornbread muffins so we should be just about ready to sit down at the table. Jama, show him where the guest bathroom is so he can wash up."

"Sure." Jama turned and smiled. "See what I told you. She likes you already."

"That doesn't count. I only made it in the door. The real test will come when we are at the table."

"Don't be silly."

"I'm not. You just wait."

She took him down a small hallway and showed him the bathroom. "I'll be in the kitchen when you get done."

"Okay."

He waited until she was gone and then washed his hands. As he went to find the kitchen he noticed an array of framed photographs hanging on the wall. He spotted Jama in a few of them. There was even a group photo of all four siblings that looked pretty recent.

"I found him." Lillian startled him. "I was afraid you got lost, but couldn't imagine where you might have wandered off to. My house isn't that large."

"Sorry. I got side-tracked by the photos."

"If you like those, I'll have to show you my large photo albums after lunch. I have three, one for each child, except Patty and Claire. As twins they've always been inseparable so their album is together. I don't ever see those two marrying unless they find a set of male twins so similar to themselves. But who knows, they may just surprise me one day."

She pointed to a picture of her son. "Darren made me proud when he found Keely and got married. I can't wait for their wedding photos to come back so I can add their picture to my collection here. Now I'm longing to begin a new album for my grandchildren. Only time will tell if Darren or Jama will have my first grandchild. I'd almost given up on her, but Lucinda has assured me there's still hope for her yet. Jama's always been my go getter girl. So serious and ever the responsible one. You can even see it in her photos."

"Yes, you can."

"But I see a difference in her today. She's more relaxed and appears happier than I've seen in a long time."

"She's trying to take more time for herself."

Lillian nodded. "That's good, but I believe there is more to the change in her than even that. I believe it's because of you, Kyle. I'm grateful to you for that. Come, the food is on the table getting cold. And Lucinda tells me her beignets must be eaten within an hour of making or they aren't worth having."

"Then lead the way."

He followed her back down the hall to the dining room. Jama and Lucinda were already seated at the table waiting on them. He took the empty place beside Jama. She reached for his hand and gave it a squeeze.

Lillian sat at the head of the table and bowed her head. "Dear Lord, thank you for this day and the friends we share this meal with. Be with my daughter and her young man. And Dear Lord, it would make me so happy to see them settled. My life would be complete if I could see at least two of my children married and with children of their own. Amen."

"Amen," Lucinda said.

"Mother!"

Jama's hold on his hand turned into a strong grip and he tensed. If she squeezed any more he was sure his fingers would lose circulation. He tried to pull his hand away, but she wouldn't let go.

"What?" Lillian smiled sweetly. "Can't I ask for what I want? The scripture tells us ask and ye shall receive."

"I knew this was a mistake bringing him here. I knew you'd think we were getting married just because I brought him home to meet you. Why are you so bent on seeing me married?"

"A mother always wants to see her child happy. Is that so wrong? You've never brought anyone home before, so why shouldn't I hope that?" Lillian calmly clasped her hands together in front of her. Her voice never wavered as she spoke. "Besides, you're wearing Keely's charm. Lucinda told me all about it. How it worked for her and Darren. Can't I assume it's doing the same for you and Kyle?"

Jama finally released his hand and stood. She reached up and took off the necklace.

Lucinda crossed herself. "You shouldn't do that, child. Put it back on now, quickly. You're messing with the all-powerful gris-gris. You don't want to do that."

"No. If what Kyle and I have is real then taking this gris-gris off will not change it." She turned to him. "Do you feel any differently about me?"

He stared at her and slowly shook his head. "Calm down. What your mom said is okay. She's not scaring me away."

"My mom shouldn't jump to conclusions about us. Maybe I don't want to get married. Maybe I want to …"

"You want to what?" he asked. Didn't she want the same things in life as he did? Surely he hadn't been wrong about her too.

"I don't know. I really don't know anymore." She sat back down and looked at the necklace lying in her hand. It wasn't glowing. It wasn't warm or hot or cold. Had she somehow broken the magic spell by taking it off? She'd been warned not to and now that she had, she feared what would happen.

Kyle reached for it and gave it back to Lucinda. "No piece of jewelry is going to change how I feel about Jama. Whether she wears that or not. I didn't fall in love with it. I fell in love with her."

"Hmm." Lucinda's brow arched. "Interesting."

Jama swiveled in her chair to face him. "You…you what?"

"I fell in love with you," he repeated, cupping her face between his hands. "Not that silly necklace you've been wearing. When you told me it had powers I didn't believe you, even if it did flash light and heat up when we kissed that time."

She smiled and moisture blurred her vision. Her voice cracked when she spoke. "Do you really?"

He nodded.

"I—I think I'm in love with you too, but I didn't want to rush it for fear of being wrong." She closed her eyes and bit her lip. "Ted…"

"I know. He hurt you just like Carol did me."

"Yes." She opened her eyes and a tear slid down her cheek.

He leaned forward and kissed her, pulling her into his arms.

Lillian cleared her throat, but neither paid any attention as they kissed.

"Well this little display of drama has been interesting," Lillian said. "Pass the mashed potatoes, Lucinda, before the meal is ruined."

Jama giggled, finally pulling away from him. "I think that's Mom's way of saying let's eat."

Lucinda handed him the roast platter.

Chapter Seventeen

Later that night as Jama prepared for bed, someone knocked on her door. Figuring it had to be Lucinda, she called, "Come in."

"Good, you are still up. I wanted to talk to you about the gris-gris." The woman came into the room wearing a flowing robe and a silk turban.

"Do you sleep like that?" Jama asked.

She touched the wrap. "Only when I'm moisturizing my hair. The summer heat can be so drying on the scalp. May I sit on the bed with you and chat?"

"Sure." Jama kicked off her slippers and crawled into the middle of the bed to sit crossed legged. "What do you have to tell me about the necklace?"

Lucinda took Jama's hand in hers and traced her lifeline with her nail. "You must wear the gris-gris again. Not for you and Kyle. But for your future. I can't explain everything; I just know that the charm has taken on a new purpose for you besides bringing you and your soul mate together. It will guide you with your business."

"My business. What do you see, Lucinda? Is my agency in trouble?"

"I see three men who want to do harm."

Jama took a deep breath. "Lynch, Higgins and Boyd?"

Lucinda shook her head. "I do not see names only figures and darkness. Those men are up to no good. The gris-gris and the crystal orb I sent you will help keep your focus on the path you must take."

"I see. And if I don't wear the charm?"

She frowned. "Why wouldn't you? You've seen firsthand how it works. What harm can wearing it do you?" Lucinda reached into her robe pocket and brought out the charm. She waved her other hand over it and chanted something Jama couldn't understand. Then she placed it in Jama's hand. "Put it on now, and do not remove it again unless I tell you to do so."

She did as she was told and the gris-gris glowed and warmed against her skin. "Is there anything else I should know?"

"Darren and Keely will arrive in the morning. They decided after your last phone conversation to return early, besides she isn't feeling too well. But all is good."

"I never meant for them to cut their trip short."

Lucinda stood. "Don't worry. She's the one who persuaded Darren to come home. Just don't mention this to Lillian. She'll be cross with me that I didn't tell her."

"Okay," Jama moved off the bed as well and turned down the covers. "I guess I better pack my things before going into the office. It will feel strange being back in my own place tomorrow night."

"No more taking care of Duke either." Lucinda winked. "Pleasant dreams."

"You too." She waited until she was alone before she went into the bathroom and brushed her teeth. If Darren and Keely were returning home, then she could definitely begin making vacation plans.

Waking early, Jama packed her suitcase, then stripped the bed and put clean sheets on it, before she got ready for work. She put on her power suit and twisted her hair onto her head, holding it in place with her favorite decorative clip. Heading out the door, she noticed the broken picture frame still lying on the chest. She'd forgotten to replace it so she made a mental note to run by the store and pick one up on her way into work hoping Keely wouldn't be too upset with her.

Lucinda was already in the kitchen, sipping coffee and eating toast when she came downstairs. "I made enough for two if you'd like a cup to go."

"Thanks. I could use one." She headed to the cabinet for her insulated mug.

"Don't be nervous. Today will go fine. You look dressed to kill. Keep a positive attitude."

"That's my plan." She glanced over her shoulder at Lucinda. "You're up early. Busy day?"

"No. I have no plans for today other than to fix Darren and Keely a nice dinner to welcome them home."

Jama went to the refrigerator and took out the bag of bagels and container of cream cheese. Taking a knife from the drawer, she split one and dropped the halves into the toaster. "You may want to consider staying with Mom to give the newlyweds some privacy."

Lucinda chuckled. "I offered, but Keely insisted there was no need before she left on her honeymoon. Still I might just do that."

When the bagel halves popped up, Jama smeared cream cheese on them before fitting them together. She slipped the bagel into a plastic bag and dropped it into her purse. Picking up her mug, she turned. "Well, I'm off."

"Drive carefully," Lucinda said. "I'll feed Duke and make sure he has water."

"Thanks." Jama pulled her suitcase out the door and closed it. She stopped by the fence to say goodbye to Duke. He lay under the tree, but got up, stretching when he saw her. "Looks like today is your lucky day, boy. Darren and Keely will be back later. You won't have to put up with me anymore."

He gave a woeful howl, throwing his head back.

"No more jogging with me. You'll be better off anyway. Take care and I'll see ya soon." She started toward her car, but stopped when he barked. Turning around she saw he'd jumped up on the chain-link fence, his front paws reaching the top bar. He barked again and wagged his tail.

Jama parked the suitcase and set her coffee mug and purse on the ground. She went back to the fence and rubbed his head. "I'll miss you too, but I've got to get to the office now. Lucinda's here. You know her. She'll feed you in a little while."

He wagged his tail and licked at her hand.

"Be a good boy."

As if he was satisfied, he jumped down from the fence and went back to the tree.

Jama swallowed the lump that formed in her throat. Why did her heart feel like it was breaking just because it was time for her to go back to her own place? She'd dreaded taking care of the dog and yet he made leaving feel horrible. She shook her head and went back to her things, gathering them before going to her car and stowing the suitcase in the trunk. Once inside she got the hand sanitizer out of her purse and used it on her hands so she could eat her breakfast as she drove into the office.

"Morning, Jama," Sue Charles greeted her as she stepped off the elevator.

She glanced at her watch and saw it wasn't even eight yet. "You're here early."

"I got a text from Keely that she'd be here later today. Their flight should land in about an hour. Did you know they'd cut their trip short by a few days."

"Lucinda told me last night."

"Lucinda is back in town too?"

"She arrived Saturday. It seems everyone is in town these days."

"Apparently. I've got to get to work."

Sue headed to her office and Jama turned toward hers. She set down her briefcase and took off her suit jacket as her phone rang. "Jama Wright."

"It's Kyle. How are you this morning?"

"Good so far. And you?"

"Thinking about our trip. Did you confirm the reservation last night?"

"Yes. And you needed the exact dates. Give me a second to open up my email and I'll have those for you. Do you have a busy day ahead?"

"A few check-ups, some shots and my monthly house call this afternoon to the assisted living place. What about you?"

"At the moment it's pretty routine for a Monday. However that could change if I get the surprise visit Lucinda warned me about. But if it happens I'm ready for them."

"Good. I'll let you go then."

"Okay." She moved her mouse over the forward tab and typed in his email address in the 'To' box before clicking on send. "I forwarded you the email confirmation of the trip."

"It just arrived in my inbox."

"Great. I'll be back at my place tonight." She paused and took a deep breath. "Keely and Darren are coming home today. I had to say goodbye to Duke this morning."

"And?"

"It wasn't easy. I'm going to miss him. A lot."

"Ah honey, it isn't like you won't be able to visit him."

"I know. But I didn't want anything to do with him and now...well," her voice cracked and she bit her lip. The lump returned to her throat and she cleared it. "I think going back to my empty condo is not going to be easy."

"You could always get a pet of your own."

She laughed. "I'm so busy. Do you think that would be fair?"

"You made time for Duke. You didn't think you had time for him, but you found it."

Kyle was right. She had made time for the dog. Maybe she could handle one of her own. "I'll think about it."

"You don't have to rush into anything either, especially before our trip."

"Yeah, it wouldn't be good to get a pet and then take off. We've both seen how a dog can react to being passed around so often."

"Duke is a prime example of it. I gotta go. Vikki just popped her head in my doorway to say that my first patient is here. Let's have dinner?"

"Okay. I'll call when I start to leave the office and you can tell me where to meet you."

"Sounds like a plan."

"Bye." She hung up smiling and turned to her computer to send her assistant an email. She'd just hit send when Pamela came to her door.

"Marketing finally sent up that feasibility report you requested."

"Great. I've been waiting on that." Jama reached for the report and glanced through the pages. "I've sent you a statement I'd like printed on company letterhead and faxed to our client list."

"Certainly. Will there be anything else?" Pamela asked.

"Yes. If Ferguson Lynch or a Mr. Boyd and Mr. Higgins show up to see me, send them to the conference room and find me immediately."

"You got it." Her assistant turned to leave.

"And Pamela, Darren and Keely are supposed to be back later this morning. Can you order flowers for her office and maybe some chocolates for his? With cards saying welcome back, love Jama. They cut their trip a few days short on account of me. I'm sure they'll say otherwise, but I have a feeling my phone call to them last week spurred their decision."

"I'm on it."

"Thanks."

She read over the report and made a few notes, pleased with the results. She hoped Kyle would be too. Once she ran over these with him tonight she could move on to phase two, getting Kit back to town to do the radio and television spots. She had enough sponsors lined up to support the young man's rodeo pursuits for at least a year.

The gris-gris warmed against her skin, startling her. She wasn't accustomed to it doing that except when she was with Kyle. But now that Lucinda said it had taken on a different purpose with her, she had to wonder what it meant.

She reached for the phone and dialed a number.

"Eastland Animal Clinic, this is Vikki. How can I help you?"

"Vikki, it's Jama Wright. How are you today?"

"Fine, Ms. Wright. How's Duke?"

"He's doing great. Listen, I need to get in touch with Kit Blankenship. I didn't get his number when we were at the McDougals. I don't suppose you have it?"

"Sure I do, but he's in Texarkana right now and the reception on his cell isn't great. He said he'd call me again when he reached Cheyenne in a couple of days. Should I have him give you a call then?"

"That will be great. I'll give you my cell number to give him so he can reach me anytime. I have his sponsorship lined up, and if he's still agreeable we can have him back in Tennessee soon."

"Fantastic. He promised to show me a few riding tricks when he comes back."

"That sounds like fun. You ready to take down my number?"

"Sure."

Jama gave her the digits and ended the call. She turned back to her computer and went into her project file on the Eastland Animal Clinic and clicked to mark off several items as complete. She saved the file and then closed it.

A knock at her open office door drew her attention. She smiled. Keely and Darren, dressed for business, stood in the doorway. "What are you doing here? Aren't you still supposed to be lounging on a beach somewhere?"

Darren laughed. "Not when I'm needed back here. Besides Keely was getting so homesick she was getting sick."

"No I wasn't. I ate some bad seafood, but I'm fine now." She shook her head and crossed her arms.

"That doesn't sound pleasant." Jama walked over to the small conference area of her office and offered them a seat. She went to the door and closed it for privacy. "I won't lie and say I'm not glad you took it upon yourself to come back when you did. There was a development over the weekend and I may need your help."

"More than what happened with Lynch?"

"Yes." She nodded, sitting in the arm chair. She briefly explained her phone call from McDaniel. And the steps she took to reassure him and Gleason as well as the statement she prepared. "Lucinda tells me to expect the men from New York to visit sometime today."

"You appear calm about this," Keely said.

"Looks can be deceiving. I'd love to know what is going on over at Jackson and Jackson. I'm sure they have spent the weekend preparing for the possibility of pouncing on my client list with the news that I'm selling."

"I still have contacts over there. I could give a call and see what I can find out," Keely offered.

"That would be great." She turned to her brother. "Darren, I was hoping you could give me further insight into what to expect from Boyd and Higgins if they should show up."

He shook his head. "It isn't what to expect but what you need to show them that will work. You don't want to appear like an unsuspecting flower waiting to be plucked. You need to hit them with stone cold facts."

"Like what?" she asked, scooting to the edge of the seat. "Should we do a quick feasibility study of the effects big business has on smaller business?"

"Great idea. But we won't have to conduct one. Before I left New York, I did a feasibility study on just that. This was for my own personal interest because I'd seen how so many of the agencies the firm had acquired slowly died. To me it didn't seem right. I guess that's the reason I became disenchanted with my job. That wasn't why I went into advertising. I was there to promote business not gobble it up and spit out the skeletal remains."

"Is that what you think they want to do to us?"

He shrugged. "Hard to say. It really depends on what Lynch told them. He obviously told them you were eager to merge or they wouldn't have just shown up here to meet with you like this. I'd say they thought you'd be delighted they paid you the compliment of coming here, and since it sounds like you didn't greet them with open arms, they may be rethinking their strategy." He took a deep breath. "Of course what I'm saying is all speculation. I have no way of knowing what Boyd and Higgins are thinking. Or if they'll even show up here."

"Lucinda was certain they would. She saw it."

Darren laughed. "When did you start believing in her nonsense?"

"It isn't nonsense," Keely interjected. "Lucinda knows what she knows."

She got up from the loveseat and went over to the bookcase, picking up the crystal orb. "Jama, where'd you get this?"

"Lucinda sent it to me. She said it would bring me clarity. If you wind it up, it plays *Some Enchanted Evening.*"

Keely did and the tune filled the office. "Not to change the subject, but did you meet your stranger?"

"You could say that."

She nodded. "Darren, Lucinda can see things. Don't forget she knew I'd meet you before we met, and I'm sure she knew Jama would meet someone. Why else would she have suggested I give the gris-gris to her?"

He shifted on the loveseat. "Okay. Point taken, but we don't need to be talking about matters of the heart right now. We need to be focusing on a strategy to get Boyd and Higgins to back off."

"My business is a matter of the heart, Darren," Jama said, standing up. She crossed her arms. "It's my baby. I've labored very hard to bring it to where it is today. I've sacrificed so much. Maybe a little too much. It was my wanting to have more freedom that tempted me into taking the meeting with Lynch. If I hadn't, then this wouldn't be happening."

"You can't blame yourself." Darren stood as well and pulled her into a hug. She hugged him back. "If we're going to start laying blame then I deserve some too. I urged you to hear Lynch out. To check into your options."

"I wish I had a camera," Keely cooed, sitting the crystal orb back on the shelf. "This is so sweet seeing you two hug. Brother and sisterly love…it makes me miss Alex."

Darren dropped his arms and Jama stepped away from him. "I'm sorry I didn't get to meet Alex at the wedding."

"You didn't miss him because he wasn't there. He had a major business trip that he couldn't get out of that had been planned a year in advance or something. Lucinda wasn't happy with him over it, but what could he do? Refuse to go and jeopardize his job? I didn't want that even if I wanted my brother at the wedding. Luckily our videographer suggested a solution. He sent Alex a live feed of the wedding. So even if he wasn't here to walk me down the aisle, Alex was able to watch from India on his laptop."

"He was in India? What kind of business is he in?"

"Environmental mineral rights. He's been working in Alaska for the last few years, though he hinted he might be coming home again because there have been rumors of another transfer for him. I hope so."

"Maybe it will happen," Jama agreed.

"Okay, back to the task at hand." Darren sat back down. "We need to put together a rough market report, pulling in information from my study as evidence that whenever a larger company tries to buy a smaller one, especially in today's economic environment, it doesn't work. The smaller business will be devalued and not worth the acquisition."

Jama nodded. "You go find that study and begin pulling data. Keely can go make a few phone calls to her contacts over at Jackson and Jackson. And I'll…" She shrugged. "Not sure what I should do."

Darren grinned. "You'll carry on your daily business until I get these figures for you and Keely makes the calls. Then we'll get back together and strategize."

"All right."

"Don't worry, Jama." Her sister-in-law smiled. "It will all work out."

She took a deep breath. "I hope you're right, Keely."

Alone again, she went back to her desk. The gris-gris grew warm against her skin and she reached up to touch it. She hoped it was warming because she was on the right path. Surely if she wasn't it would be turning cold in warning. At least that is how it had worked where Kyle had been concerned.

The thought of Kyle reminded her about the report on her desk. She buzzed Pamela. "Did marketing send up more than one copy of this report?"

"Yes."

"Good. I need it sent by courier to the Eastland Animal Clinic. I'll email you a cover letter to go along with it."

"Okay. Mr. Lynch just called and said he'd be coming by in an hour to meet with you. He asked that you clear your schedule."

"He called? I hadn't expected any warning from him. Thanks."

She hung up and quickly typed up the cover letter explaining the highlights of the report and sent it to Pamela. Then she dug in her briefcase and pulled out the packet Boyd and Higgins had given her on Friday night. She went to Darren's office. He had the sleeves on his dress shirt rolled up to his elbows, and he was eating a piece of chocolate while he worked.

"Sorry to bother you, but I remembered this and thought it might help with your analysis. Also, Lynch just called. They'll be here in an hour."

"He called?" Darren's brows arched.

"That was my reaction too."

"Hmmm. I'll take a look at this and see if there are any surprises hidden within the wording that we should worry about."

"Thanks."

"Thank you for the chocolates. That was nice."

"Just my way was saying you are valued around here, little brother."

Darren laughed and reached for another piece of chocolate.

Chapter Eighteen

Jama paced back and forth from one end of her office to the other keeping an eye on the clock as she waited for Lynch and his guests to arrive. Her confidence level was high, yet she noted an also high level of nervous energy coursing through her veins. Darren's marketing report and quick visual aids proved their point, and she hoped Boyd and Higgins would bow out without retribution. That's what worried her the most. Would there be reprisal for turning them down?

The phone's intercom buzz made her jump and she hurried over to the desk. "Yes, Pamela?"

"Your guests are waiting in the conference room."

Jama took a deep breath. "Please ask Keely and Darren to join me there."

"Yes, Ms. Wright."

She slipped her suit jacket on, picked up her folio pad and pen, and headed to the conference room. Darren and Keely were waiting at the conference door for her.

"Smile," he urged. "We've got this."

Nodding, she opened the door and entered. "Good day, gentlemen."

Mr. Boyd and Mr. Higgins stood and shook hands with them.

"Good to see you again, Darren."

"Likewise. This is my wife, Keely Jones."

"Gentlemen." Keely smiled, taking a seat at the table.

"So what do I owe the pleasure of this visit?" Jama asked, sitting at the head of the table. She glanced at Lynch who'd remained seated. He wore a stern look, and she wondered if he suspected this meeting wasn't going in his favor.

"We wanted to follow up with you before we left town. To see if you'd made a decision."

Her forced smile hurt the longer she kept it. "Really? How kind of you, especially since Mr. Lynch was telling every client of mine he ran into after I left Friday evening that I was selling to you. I don't appreciate having lies spread about me. I wasn't interested in selling and after Mr. Lynch's treachery I will not be agreeing to anything."

"We weren't aware of what Mr. Lynch told others." Mr. Boyd tapped his pen on the table. "We're sorry for that. But please don't base your decision on his actions."

"Whether you knew or not isn't important." Jama stood and Darren passed around the photo-copied visual aids he'd put together. "My decision to not merge is also based on research of local business. That is my client base, gentlemen. Studies show that firms with primary local business when merged with an outside larger business nine times out of ten will result in failure over the long-term. Your agency has seen this. You've gone in and acquired smaller ones that failed and in return you have nothing to show for your investment. I'm sure taking a loss is nothing for big business and it benefits your firm tax wise, but for a small business like mine, it would ruin me.

"I've worked long and hard to keep Wright & Associates' head above water these last few years and I'm not about to let anything pull it down again. As much as having financial backing from a larger firm appeals, I'm not willing to take on the risk of eventual failure. A few of my clients have already expressed their plans to leave if I were to sell. If they do then I'm sure it is only a matter of time before more follow. As I see it, Wright & Associates would be taking a downhill spiral."

"I'd like to say you are making a big mistake, Ms. Wright, but I won't," Mr. Higgins smiled. "Merging is not right for everyone. We did our research on the agencies in the area and felt yours was strong enough to withstand the trials of a merger before Mr. Lynch contacted you. However, if your client base is so opposed then it will not benefit you or Crabtree, Boyd and Lane to merge. We're here to expand our business, like you, having learned from the mistakes of our parent company."

"I'm glad to hear that," Darren said. "And I'm sorry this couldn't work out."

"It's all business." Mr. Boyd stood and offered her his hand. "We wish you much success, Ms. Wright."

Jama blinked and shook hands with him. They'd pulled it off. They'd really pulled it off. Tingles ran up her spine and she smiled. "Thank you for understanding."

Mr. Higgins stood and shook her hand as well before turning to Darren. "We told your sister we weren't here to steal you away, but if you ever get tired of the smaller business and want to return to New York, the door is always open."

"Thank you for the offer. At present I'm happy here, but I'll remember your offer."

"There would be a place for you as well, Ms. Jones. We're quite aware of your success with Jackson and Jackson before you came here. You've created a name for yourself."

"Thank you for the compliment. Can I walk you to the elevator, gentlemen?" Keely offered.

As soon as Higgins and Boyd were gone, Darren shut the conference room door, preventing Lynch from leaving. "I think you owe my sister an apology."

"As the men said, it's all business." He stood and offered her his hand. "No hard feelings."

"I'm afraid that doesn't cut it, Lynch." Jama crossed her arms ignoring his gesture. "You had a reputation in town and after this stunt it will be even worse. Don't come sniffing around my company again, no matter what opportunity you hear about. Is that clear?"

He dropped his hand down to his side again. "Crystal. Now if you'll excuse me, I have an appointment."

"I still did not hear an apology." Darren stood in front of the door and did not move.

Lynch pursed his lips together and turned to Jama. "I'm sorry for spreading falsehoods about your company. Can you really fault me for telling what I thought were future truths? How could I know you were going to turn them down?"

"Future truths?" Jama smirked. "I hope you don't base all your business moves on those because this one came back to bite you in the butt, Lynch. Now get out of here and don't come back."

Darren opened the door and stepped out of the man's way.

"We did it!!" Jama clapped her hands and danced in place. "And it wasn't even as hard as I feared."

"Are you saying you doubted the gris-gris?" Darren asked.

Jama stood still again and reached up, touching the charm. It was warm. "No. But I thought I'd have to work harder to win this victory. Do you think our presentation made that big a difference to them?"

"I think it showed them you were a force to be reckoned with and you were not some naïve CEO." Darren went to the conference table and picked up the visual aids. "Plus, did you not see Lynch's reaction when I walked into the room? The blood literally drained from his face. Boyd and Higgins were surprised too. Those men knew they were beat."

"Are we celebrating yet?" Keely asked, coming back into the room. She handed Darren a cream colored business card. "Mr. Higgins said I should give you this."

"Embossed with gold lettering." He tossed the card on the table with the visual aid materials. "Who's he trying to impress?"

"Obviously us. He offered me a corner office if I persuaded you to come join them, but I told him no thanks. I already had one here and I wanted my babies raised right here, not in a high-rise apartment."

Jama smiled. "Babies?"

Keely shrugged. "Well anything could happen."

"Just because Lucinda told you they'd be a bundle of joy in our lives within the first year does not mean we're having a baby." Darren shook his head and smirked.

"Wait a minute. Lucinda told me Keely had been sick but that it was all good."

"She was sick and throwing up."

"Because I ate bad seafood. There were others at the hotel who had been to the same restaurant and ate the same dish as me who were sick. The resort doctor confirmed it."

"Okay. No need to argue over it. Keely asked if we were celebrating. And I think we should. I'm going to go call Kyle and have him join us. Why don't you two take a long lunch and when you return we'll pop the cork on a bottle of champagne?"

"Excellent idea." Keely slipped her arm around Darren's. "Maybe we should run home and check on Duke."

"Sure. It will be nice to see how he's doing."

Once they left, Jama picked up her portfolio and pen, then remembered Lucinda was at the house. She hurried to catch them at the elevator, but it had already closed. She tried Darren on his cell, but it went to voice mail. So did Keely's. Oh well, they'd find out soon enough that they weren't alone.

Chapter Nineteen

Jama stood at her bookcase looking at the crystal orb sometime later trying to see what fascination others had with it, other than its beauty. Lucinda kept telling her it would bring clarity, but she didn't understand how. Was there magic in the music? She cranked the little handle and listened to the song once more.

A knock at her door sounded and she put the orb back on the bookshelf. Turning she saw Kyle and butterflies fluttered in her stomach. "You found me. Did you have any trouble?"

"No, your directions were perfect. Vikki said it was urgent I come as soon as my schedule cleared. What's up?"

"Come in and shut the door and I'll tell you." She smiled, walking toward him. "Wright & Associates is out of jeopardy. The dilemma from the weekend has been taken care of and everything is fine again. As soon as Keely and Darren get here we're going to celebrate."

"I'm so happy things worked out for you," Kyle said, wrapping his arms around her waist. "I'm also glad you wanted to include me in the celebration."

"I couldn't wait to share the news with you. I called, but Vikki said you were tied up with a patient. It sounds like business is picking up for the clinic already."

"Yeah. I got the report you sent over."

"We can talk about that later. And what that means for your campaign."

"Good," he leaned his head toward hers, and she tilted her face up to him for a kiss. He pulled her closer and parted her lips with his tongue, exploring the depths of her mouth.

She closed her eyes, returning his kiss. She ran her hands up his back, spearing her fingers into his hair above his shirt collar. A moan escaped her throat and her pulse quickened. The gris-gris burned hot against her flesh.

"Jama?"

At the sound of Darren's voice, she pulled away from Kyle and they both turned toward the door. Her brother's frown indicated he was unhappy by what he'd walked in on.

"Sorry to interrupt. Pamela said we should come on in, that you were waiting for us," Keely explained. "Maybe we should come back later."

"No. Come on in," Jama urged. "Kyle, you know Keely already, but you haven't met my brother, Darren. Darren, this is Kyle Landers. Duke's vet and my boyfriend."

A light flashed from the gris-gris.

"It's nice to meet you, Darren," Kyle said, offering his hand.

"Likewise." Darren returned the gesture. "What are your intentions with my sister?"

"Darren!" Jama shook her head. "He already met mother. He doesn't have to receive the third degree from you."

"It's okay, Jama. I understand what his concerns are because of your past relationships. I'm not Ted if that is what you're worried about. I want only the best for Jama."

"I think this is wonderful," Keely cooed. She stepped toward her husband and took his hand. "Don't you agree, darling?"

Darren nodded. "If you hurt her, I'll hurt you."

Jama rolled her eyes. "Geez. I think I can take care of myself here. And just so you know, Kyle and I are taking a vacation together in four weeks. That gives you plenty of time to adjust to it and get over this protector-of-the-universe attitude."

"Are you out of your mind?"

"Maybe, but I'm doing it so get over it, little brother."

Jama walked over to her desk and picked up a plastic bag and handed it to Keely. "Sorry about your picture frame. I knocked it off trying to get the phone the night Mr. Brubaker called about Duke's howling. I didn't get to replace it until today."

"I wondered what happened. Thanks."

She buzzed her assistant. "Pamela, we're ready for the champagne. Please let Sue and Judith know."

"Yes, Ms. Wright."

Jama walked back to Kyle and he wrapped his arm around her waist. "I'm happy, Darren. That should be the most important thing."

He nodded. "Okay."

The door opened and Pamela walked in with a large ice bucket containing two bottles of champagne. Sue followed carrying a tray of crystal flutes and Judith brought up the rear with a glass platter of fruit, cheese, and crackers.

"Darren, will you do the honors and pop the cork on the first bottle?" Jama asked. When each person had a filled flute, she continued. "We are here to celebrate the success of Wright & Associates being in the black for over a year, the marriage of my brother and Keely, and the future whatever it may bring."

"Here. Here." Keely raised her glass in a toast, clinking her glass with Darren's before they took a sip.

Jama turned to Kyle and kissed him. "I love you."

He smiled. "Are you sure? As your brother pointed out you've only known me for three weeks."

She nodded. "I think I've loved you since that trip to the ER."

He set his untouched flute on the small table and did the same with hers. He led her to the opposite side of the room and cupped her face with his hands, brushing his lips against hers. "I know I have."

She smiled. "Meeting you has made my life complete."

"Marrying you would make mine." His tone was serious and the look in his eyes was as well.

Her heart fluttered and her knees felt weak. *Was he really asking what it sounded like?* "Yes."

"Are you agreeing or saying yes?"

"Yes…I'm saying yes. Nothing would make me happier than to be Mrs. Kyle Landers."

He laughed and pulled her into his arms, lifting her off the ground and turning around with her. Jama threw her head back and laughed too.

"What's going on?" Darren asked.

"Oh phooey, we're too late," Lillian said as she walked into the office with Lucinda.

"Too late for what?" He turned and looked at his mother. "What are you doing here?"

"You're sister is getting married." Lillian wiped moisture from her eyes and hugged him. "I couldn't be happier."

"Married?"

"Looks like we have more to celebrate, ladies." Keely took the open bottle of champagne and refilled all the glasses. "Let's toast this time to Kyle and Jama."

"The gris-gris worked again," Sue said, munching on cheese cubes.

"It always works, my dear." Lucinda winked and came over to talk to her. "You're Keely's assistant, am I right?"

"Yes ma'am. Sue Charles."

"And you're single?"

"Unfortunately."

"Maybe things will change."

"A girl can only hope."

Lucinda laughed and went over to Jama and Kyle. "Congratulations to you both."

"Thank you. You were right about everything." Jama hugged her.

"Of course I was. Now, it's time you give me the gris-gris back."

Jama laid her hand on the charm. "Already? But you said last night I shouldn't take it off again until you said—"

Lucinda nodded. "Yes. It has done all it needs to do for you. It has much work to do for another now."

"Okay." Jama reluctantly removed the charm. She kissed it and gave it to Lucinda. "You know the blood red stone didn't spill forth for me."

"It didn't have to. You believed in its powers so it didn't have to prove itself to you. That is the reason its purpose changed from finding your soul mate to helping you secure your future. I believe it did that fully today."

"Who will you give it to next?"

"That will be revealed soon. Don't you worry."

Lucinda's Beignets

Ingredients:

- 1½ cups lukewarm water
- ½ cup granulate sugar
- 1 envelope active dry yeast
- 2 eggs, slightly beaten
- 1 ¼ teaspoons salt
- 1 cup evaporated milk
- 7 cups bread flour (or you can substitute all-purpose flour)
- ¼ cup shortening
- Nonstick spray
- Oil for deep-frying
- 3 cups confectioners' sugar

Directions:

Mix water, sugar, and yeast in a large bowl and let sit for 10 minutes.

In a mixing bowl (stand up mixer with dough hook), beat eggs, salt, and evaporated milk together. Mix egg mixture to the yeast mixture. In a separate bowl, measure out the bread flour. Add 3 cups of the flour to the yeast mixture and stir to combine. Add the shortening and continue to stir while adding the remaining flour. Remove dough from the bowl, place on a lightly floured surface and knead until smooth. Spray a large bowl with nonstick spray. Put dough into bowl and cover with plastic wrap or a towel. Let rise in a warm place for at least 2 hours.

Preheat oil in a deep-fryer to 350 degrees F. (if dough doesn't rise immediately to top when dropped in, the oil isn't hot enough.)

Add the confectioners' sugar to a paper or plastic bag and set aside.

Roll the dough out to ¼-inch thickness and cut into 1-inch squares. Slid squares into oil slowly to avoid splattering. Deep-fry, flipping constantly, for 2-3 minutes until they become a golden color. After beignets are fried, drain them for a few seconds on paper towels, and then toss them into the bag of confectioners' sugar. Hold bag closed and shake to coat evenly. Serve while still warm.

Unused dough can be kept for up to 1 week in refrigerator. Just punch down when it rises. Also, you can freeze dough; roll and cut pieces before freezing.

A special sneak peak
Book #3
The Good Luck Series

The Good Luck Potion

Leanne Tyler

Chapter One

Alex carried the last cardboard box from his truck into the house and set it on the kitchen counter. He surveyed the room and shook his head. Keely had given the kitchen her own personal touch, removing all memory of their mom while she lived here the last three years. She'd even stripped off the wallpaper and painted. He couldn't really blame her. But the kitchen had been the one room in the house that he had tried to leave the same to preserve their mother's memory. Perhaps he should have mentioned that before he left for Alaska.

A light knock sounded at the back door before it opened and his sister walked in. "Hey. Are you all settled in?"

He smiled, noticing the loose fitting top she wore trying to conceal evidence that he was going to have a niece or nephew in a few months. "Almost. What about you? Have you and Darren finished unpacking at your new house?"

"He's going through the last box of books for the office. I, on the other hand, just finished in the kitchen and was getting ready to make dinner when I realized I must have left my favorite casserole dish behind. Do you mind if I check the cabinets?"

"You can't cook without it?"

"No...well yes...but it's the right size for what I'm making tonight."

He chuckled. "You sound like Mom. Remember how she had to have that certain bowl whenever she mixed her stuffing at Thanksgiving? She was convinced it wouldn't taste the same otherwise."

"I totally get where she was coming from now that I do so much cooking." Keely opened a cabinet door and squatted down to peer inside. "Just as I thought. I should have never let Darren help me pack up the kitchen. He totally missed this cabinet. Is that box empty? My casserole dish is not the only item we left."

Alex quickly emptied the box of its contents and watched her pull out several platters and large, colorful round dish with several small compartments.

"What is that?"

"It's a relish plate. It's great for when you're having company and are doing a fruit platter or a Mexican night. Guacamole can go in the center while you fill the rest with sour cream, cheese, peppers, onion, lettuce, chunks of tomatoes."

He shook his head. "You've become so domesticated."

"Getting married does that to a person. Help me up, won't you?"

Alex placed his hands under her arms and lifted. "How much longer do you have?"

"Four months according to the doctor, but Lucinda says it will be closer to five."

"Don't tell me she's been doing her hocus pocus on you?"

Keely laughed, rubbing her stomach. "No. She said she could tell by the way I'm carrying the baby. Why? Has she been doing it on you?"

He didn't like the way her brow arched when she asked that question. He still hadn't figured out what he was supposed to do with the tiny bottle Lucinda had given him when she paid an unexpected visit last month. In fact, her appearing unannounced and then performing the ritual before she gave it to him bordered on cryptic. Keely might believe in Lucinda's voodoo talk, not him. Did he dare tell his sister about it? Would she laugh? Or would she understand and put his concerns to rest?

"Alex?"

"Lucinda came to see me."

"She did?"

He nodded.

"Funny. She didn't mention it." Keely turned to the counter and packed the box with her dishes. When she turned back her brows were knitted together. "Though she did get called to fill in for a singer on one of those cruise ships, but she never told me it was going to Alaska. Did you have a nice visit?"

He grunted. "You know Lucinda, she's always talking mumbo jumbo, waving her hands in the air, and burning incense."

"It isn't mumbo jumbo, Alex. And please, don't let her ever hear you talk like that, it would hurt her feelings."

"Don't tell me you buy into it? All her talk about finding your true love and soul mate?"

Keely shrugged and smiled. "It doesn't matter if I believe or not. It's what you believe, little brother. I've found my perfect match and we're very happy. Maybe it's time you did the same."

Alex turned to the counter where he'd emptied the contents of the box and picked up the bottle Lucinda had given him. He weighed it in his hand, debating on asking the question that had been on his mind since he arrived home, but had almost been afraid of what Keely would answer. When he turned back to his sister, he found her watching him closely.

"Have you ever seen this before?" He held the vial.

She shook her head. "That's a pretty bottle. Where did you get it?"

"Lucinda gave it to me. She asked me to keep it safe until the time was right."

"Did she say what's in it?"

"A potion. A good luck potion."

Keely smiled. "Then you better do what she said. Keep it safe until the time is right."

"How will I know that?"

She chuckled. "You'll know. Believe me, you'll figure it out."

He set the bottle back on the counter.

"Carry the box out to my car for me. I need to get home and fix dinner. Want to come by in about an hour and eat with us?" She walked to the door.

"Love to, but I've got plans with some old friends. You remember Brandon and Phil who I played basketball with all the time."

"Yeah. How are they?" She held the door for him to exit.

"Phil's engaged. His fiancée is throwing a small party for some friends."

"You better be careful. One thing I know about couples, they love to see other couples formed out of their single friends."

181

It was his turn to chuckle. "I don't think Phil would let his fiancée do that to us."

Keely walked over to the fence and called to Duke, his overweight bloodhound. He slowly got to his feet from where he'd been lying under the shade tree. He jumped up on the fence for her to pet him. "Hello, boy. How ya doing? Miss me already?"

"He's been moping around all afternoon."

"Give him a day or two. He'll forget Darren and me and he'll be your dog again. It took a few days for him to get over spending so much time with Jama and Kyle when we returned from our honeymoon."

"I guess." Alex walked to her car and put the box in on the backseat. "Make Darren get that out for you."

"Don't worry. He will," she assured, rubbing Duke's head one last time before leaving the fence. "He's more protective of me than a mother hen of her chicks right now."

"He loves you." Alex opened the car door for her. "So do I. You drive carefully and watch out for Mr. Brubaker. He made a point of letting me know he was glad I was back so there'd be peace and quiet around here again."

Keely laughed, turning the key in the ignition. "He got his knickers in a twist while Jama stayed here and still hasn't got them unwound. Throw a loud party and make him regret saying that, won't you."

"I'll think about it." Alex shut her door and waved as she drove away. He walked to the fence where Duke stood watching her go. "She'll be back to visit. Don't look so sad. I'm here now and it's going to be like old times. You'll see."

Duke yawned and returned to the shade of the tree.

Going back in the house, Alex thought about Keely's warning as he got ready for the party. Phil had mentioned they were going to play the lock and key game tonight. He'd never heard of it, but he guessed he'd soon find out if it works.

About The Author

Award winning author, Leanne Tyler lives in the South and her writing reflects her heritage. She writes Sweet and somewhat Sensual Southern romances whether historical or contemporary. Leanne's debut release **Victory's Gate** was the 2007 American Rose winner of the Through the Garden Gate contest and was released electronically by The Wild Rose Press in December 2007. Finally in December 2009 the *Through the Garden Gate Anthology* became available in print and includes the four winning entries.

Stepping into the Contemporary circle, she debuted with her Class of '85 Reunion story *It's Always Been You* in August 2011. And her first full-length historical novel *Season of Love* (Nov. 2011) is a time-travel set in 1850 Charleston, SC. A recent release from Books to Go Now *A Country Kitchen Christmas* (Feb. 2012) is a light inspirational romance. Later this year, a short story entitled *Ava* will be released as part of the *Love Letters Series*. Another full-length historical novel *Because of Rebecca* is under contract.

She invites readers to step into her world and enjoy the passion.

You can find Leanne Tyler on the web at:
leannetyler.com or on Facebook, Twitter, Goodreads, LinkedIn, Pinterest and other social media sites.

CPSIA information can be obtained at www.ICGtesting.com
Printed in the USA
LVOW051807230513

335266LV00001B/117/P